'My Dream'

Meverly A. Benjamin

'My Dream'

By Meverly A. Benjamin

© 2018 Meverly A. Benjamin

ISBN: 9781912092536

First published in 2018 by Arkbound Ltd (Publishers)

No part of this publication may be reproduced, stored in a retrieval system, or transmitted, in any form or by any means without the prior permission of the publisher, nor be otherwise circulated in any form of binding or cover other than that in which it is published and without a similar condition being imposed on the subsequent purchaser.

Arkbound is a social enterprise that aims to promote social inclusion, community development and artistic talent. It sponsors publications by disadvantaged authors and covers issues that engage wider social concerns. Arkbound fully embraces sustainability and environmental protection. It endeavours to use material that is renewable, recyclable or sourced from sustainable forest.

Arkbound
Backfields House
Upper York Street
Bristol BS2 8QJ
England

www.arkbound.com

Table of Contents

Chapter One - The Birth And Raising Of A Dreamer 1

Chapter Two - Moving Up And Getting On 13

Chapter Three - Finding love and facing loss 23

Chapter Four - Possibilities beckon and wings are spread ... 33

Chapter Five - A new challenge and a new decision 45

Chapter Six - New love and old love and a friend in trouble 55

Chapter Seven - Coming Home 65

Chapter Eight - Home again, new start, new love 75

Chapter Nine - Married Life, Married Strife 85

Chapter Ten - Almost an end and a ne beginning 95

Chapter Eleven - New Life and New Hope 105

Chapter Twelve - The downward spiral 115

Chapter Thirteen - Rock Bottom 125

Chapter Fourteen - Through the valley of death 135

Chapter Fifteen - The road from despair 145

Chapter Sixteen - Delivering the Dream 155

Chapter Seventeen 163

References 168

Introduction

Life in itself doesn't always treat us fairly; it can often involve less funfair, and more warfare. But this warfare is not waged against witches and wizards, or against opposing countries. It's not warfare against unfavorable weather or climatic conditions, or even against economic depression.

So, what is this warfare about? What is this war we need to wage?

This warfare is an attack that attempts to derail us and ensure that we do not accomplish our reason for living. It's a battle that aims at hindering the discovery, pursuit, and fulfillment of our God-given purpose.

Enjoyment of life can only come with the attainment of our purpose and assignment, and the realisation of the dreams that cry out for fulfillment. This is your purpose.

The enemy is aware of the magnitude and the challenge of the great and mighty things that lie in wait for us when we are in the place of purpose, and because this needs to be thwarted at all costs, he wages war against us.

My Dream is the story of the war waged by a young lady, Esther, that focusses on how her courageous struggle and fight eventually led her to the discovery and fulfillment of her own purpose.

George Bernard Shaw said:

'This is the true joy in life, being used for a purpose recognized by yourself as a mighty one. Being a force of nature instead of a feverish, selfish little clod of ailments and grievances, complaining that the world will not devote itself to making you happy.'

Isaiah 26:3

"You, Lord give perfect peace to those who keep their purpose firm and put their trust in you."

When this warfare is won, the rewards are a discovery of one's purpose and the beginning of self-fulfillment.

Now, I invite you to journey through Esther's story, a story that ended with her finding her God-given purpose. At the end of this journey, I sincerely hope and believe that not only will you be inspired and motivated to confront and fight your own war, but also that you will be able to lay hold on God's plan and purpose for your life.

Chapter One

The Birth and Raising of A Dreamer

It was far from the joyous arrival into the world that was being witnessed elsewhere up and down the labour ward, on a warm first day of May in 1992. As fathers proudly passed newly delivered bundles to grandparents and exhausted mothers basked in the admiration and adoration of their husbands and relatives, one child slipped into the world almost unnoticed.

Her mother, Ruth, had been abandoned by Esther's father before her birth. Besides the overwhelming love of a mother for her newborn child, another emotion clawed at Ruth; fear of the future, the dread of being alone, of bearing the responsibility for this helpless little scrap of humanity by herself. No balloons with "it's a girl' emblazoned on them danced above the bed and not one teddy with a pink note of congratulations around its neck nestled in the corner of her baby girl's crib. Esther Washington had only her mother, and her mother only had Esther Washington.

The way that these things invariably go, Esther and her mother survived and the little girl thrived under the tutelage of a devoted and loving mother and the occasional acts of kindness from strangers that were like diamonds stumbled upon in a field of dirt. The father of baby Esther was back in Africa, an ocean and a world apart from the tiny child that he had given life to.

Sometimes Esther's mother would look down into the perfect and exquisitely beautiful face of her sleeping child and wonder how his heart would not be torn in two, being apart from the miracle they had created between them. Men, it seems, are different. Something to do with the fact that they do not actually carry the perfect creatures they create, possibly?

The young Esther blossomed and grew like a precious flower. She once heard one of the churchwomen talking to her mother, saying:

"Esther is a precious girl, she is beautiful, inside and out."

At the time, Esther thought that was a funny thing to say. How could the lady know what her insides looked like? Later she would learn that a glimpse of what someone has on the inside is not so much a glimpse at their internal organs as the shade of their heart. Some black hearts hide behind very attractive exteriors. But the child Esther was a beautiful child, her face shining with the kind of goodness and kindness that could only come from within.

Her life was hard, although she was not aware of that. Her life was her life. After a brief reconciliation just before the millennium between her mother and father, a brother, Levi, joined her but the reality of life with a lot of bills and not a lot of money frightened her father off and he left, this time for good.

Levi was sweet and together Esther and her mother tended to him. He was their little miracle and this time, as he settled into the world, there was a sister to peer in wonder into his crib, barely able to contain her excitement and dying to be given the chance to hold his tiny body wrapped in its blue hospital blanket. His skin was light and his hair a mixture of African tight curl and a softer curl. He was beautiful. His bright brown eyes stared up at his sister as she held out her little finger and he wrapped a tiny hand around it. Their bond, made in that moment, would be tested, but never broken.

Life for the family was not easy, but hard work and faith can work miracles, and it did.

Ruth worked at several menial jobs just to make sure her children had access to the basic things of life. As Esther grew older, the consciousness of what her mother was going through just to raise them became clearer. The knowledge and the gratitude for her mother's devotion and hard work matured the child beyond her years.

By the age of nine, she was helping her mother carry out domestic chores, cooking and other aspects of her official duties as an order picker, which she brought home. Esther had a multi-faceted life; she was a daughter, a helping hand, an assistant child raiser and a school pupil. Esther was an elderly young girl.

Childhood days are supposed to be carefree - that would be the ideal. However, while Esther's life was a lot better than that of other children, such as those who suffered abuse or neglect perhaps, it had its responsibilities. It came with a weight that should never rest on the shoulders of a young girl.

Through all the trials and tribulations of her young life, one thing was constant, like an umbrella protecting her from the worst of the weather, Esther had her faith. Ruth raised her children the only way that she knew how, and with the only constant that she knew would never change; the love of God. Every Sunday, the family would be in church, luxuriating in the love of those who, like them, loved the Lord. Esther became a gifted and passionate Sunday school teacher.

She threw herself into the life of the bigger family she had grown up with in the church and became a language interpreter, as well as a very active member of the ladies fellowship. Esther's desire to know God for herself led her to attend Bible study meetings, and prayer meetings too. The light of her faith guided her through the days of her life and during difficult times, it shone brighter.

Her friends loved Esther but they recognized in her an old soul. Childhood without responsibility was a luxury that Esther could not afford. While they were going to buy makeup, she was going to pay utility bills. While they were trying to wheedle more money out of their parents for things that are essential to teenage girls, Esther was trying to keep her own demands, even for the basics, to a minimum to save taxing her mother's limited resources.

If childhood is measured by the fact that it is a time without worry, without responsibility, then Esther did not have a childhood. But she did have love.

Sometimes it seemed to Esther that she was living her life on the edge of other peoples existences, that she was watching them enjoy things that she could not. It reminded her a bit of the fairytale that her mother used to read to her when she was a little girl, Cinderella, where the poor girl was left to everyday drudgery while her sisters enjoyed parties and balls and being wined and dined. They enjoyed the good life, the excitement and the thrills of life while poor Cinders sat in the fireplace cleaning and keeping the house for them.

It was not that Esther resented the work that she did, alongside her mother, to keep the home together. She did not. She was proud of her role in bringing Levi up to be a clever and inquisitive youngster who always had a smile on his face and a football under his arm. Making ends meet was a challenge to Esther and she would often leave the table still hungry so that her little brother could eat the remainder of her meal.

When her mother came in, worn out from her last job of the day, it gave Esther pleasure that the house was clean and tidy and the washing and ironing done so that all her mother had to do was sit down in a chair as Esther served her a meal on a tray. Often, Esther would have to wake her mother to eat the food, Ruth was so exhausted that she would fall asleep as soon as she sat down. Sometimes Esther would gaze at her mother's sleeping face in the same way that her mother had once looked down at the baby Esther's face, and think how beautiful her mother looked without the worry and the frown that almost seemed to pass as a permanent feature on her waking face.

They were a good team, Ruth and Esther, and just when it seemed that they were running on empty, Sunday would come around and Esther would feel the warmth of love and community refuel her for the week ahead. Given how close they all were in their church family, during the week they barely saw each other. Life was hard for most and it was all they could do to keep their head above water and food on the table.

School was an escape of sorts and Esther did enjoy being a child from the sound of the school bell in the morning to the time that she resumed her duties at home in the afternoon. Taking Levi by the hand, they would walk back through grimy streets that smelled of poverty and degradation. Once as they were coming home, a street fight broke out.

Esther saw the flash of blades and grabbing Levi tighter by the hand, ran for their lives. Levi was craning his neck to see what was going on. "Cool!" He shouted and Esther felt a wave of fear for her brother wash over her. She knew how damaging gangs could be. Friends had lost brothers to knife crime. The thought of Levi being sucked in was horrific. For the first time, Esther realized the enormity of what life on their rung of the ladder would be. Whatever she and her mother did at home and in church, however much they loved and protected Levi, he was always going to be vulnerable to the influence of others around him.

She had seen the young lads between childhood and manhood, their uncertainty making them prime victims for those who would prey on the vulnerable, and hence easy to influence individuals. She was determined to keep Levi out of the mess that sprawled their neighbourhood.

At school, Esther would join in with the banter about makeup, music and the things that occupy girls. Hairstyles and pop stars were something she could talk about although her own hair did not lend itself to many different styles. She knew that her face was beautiful since her friends reassured her of that all the time. Her eyes were dark with long lashes and a sort of definition that would only usually be achieved by expert application of eyeliner. Her cheeks showed high cheekbones and her lips were full and lush. Her friends agreed that she did not even need makeup. Just as well really, as Esther could not afford it.

As Esther grew, her body developed and her figure, that she often kept under wraps in a school uniform one size too big, was as breathtaking as her lovely face. Whereas her friends advertised their wares in tight, figure-hugging clothes and skirts that were so short their underwear was on show, Esther preferred not to be oggled. She knew that she looked out of place beside her friends and they teased her constantly, gently and not so gently trying to get her to join them in their fashion statement, to roll the waistband of her school skirt over so that her skirt would fall just below her bottom. With quite some good humour, Esther would always refuse and her friends found a reason to lover her anyway.

They knew that she was a shining star amongst them, that if she did dress as they did, no one would give them a second glance. Esther was that rare person who was breathtakingly lovely but did not know it.

When she was twelve, she heard two male classmates talking about her and the mathematics test that she had missed. They thought Esther had been playing truant and did not care about her studies.

The problem was Esther had started her menstrual periods. It was a source of great embarrassment to Esther that other people would come to realize the monthly significance of her missing lessons, but the pain and discomfort forced her to stay at home. Esther still remembered it as if it had happened yesterday. She had hated each month-end when the dreaded monster would come lurking again. At twelve years old, Esther's mother told her, "You are a woman now and you should not play with boys. Do not let any boy see this; they will laugh at you...."

Esther was confused. Most, if not all, of her all of her friends were girls and she always played with her brother. The science teacher at school had told them only that one of the changes that happen to girls as they mature is to bleed from the vagina. He gave no other information about menstruation. Most of the science teachers in school were men and none of them got into issues of reproductive health in their teaching, even though it was part of the syllabus.

The girls were referred to their textbooks to learn about their bodies and reproductive system. While they struggled to understand what was happening to their bodies, they also had to deal with the reality of managing their periods. Esther had a very heavy flow and more often than not she was in pain. The first two days were always the worst because of the severe cramps. Her menstrual periods lasted for five days, a period that felt like the longest days of her life.

Esther hated going to school during this time. Each month Esther would ask her mother for sanitary towels. She was not very comfortable during this period and hated having to sit and wait for everybody to leave the classroom before she could go out and clean up. While the teacher and the other students were busy with the lesson, Esther would be worrying about how she was going to get to the toilets without people noticing her bloodstained dress. What made matters worse was the fact that she had to walk a long distance home with 'pads' wedged uncomfortably between her legs. She often wished there could be a different time set aside for menstruating girls to go to the toilet so that they could have some privacy.

Apart from boys who were always interested in the girls' toilets, there were also other girls whose main aim was to tease and ridicule others in the toilet. Esther dreaded going to the toilets during break time, especially when she was menstruating. Esther could not concentrate on the lessons during this time of the month, which meant that she paid more attention to her bleeding at the expense of her schoolwork, often worried about when the discomfort would end. Looking back, these memories made her laugh, she knew now it was all part of the painful process of becoming a woman.

But the male of the species is not that easily fooled by attempts to camouflage appearance. Teenage boys with testosterone coursing through their veins are hard-wired to identify the finest of female forms and Esther did not go unnoticed despite her attempts to camouflage her developing body.

Meanwhile, Esther enjoyed football and any other game that involved team play. She had boys as neighbours and she played games with them, delighting in the times she won and learning from the times she did not. Esther was a team player, driven by targets. Despite her soft and gentle nature, she would be aggressive when she wanted to achieve results, and when she was part of a team.

But now the boys that she played against in sporting events were noticing her as a woman, rather than a wiry determined little fighter. Men and boys attempted to get her to give in to them, but with the help of God, she never did.

There were times of pressing financial needs, for Esther and her family, when men were willing to give much more than was needed financially, if only Esther would give herself to them in bed. Esther always declined bluntly. She was determined to stay a virgin until she was married, and with her steely determination, she achieved this.

Pushing the boys away, however, came with its share of miseries. Coupled with the effects of a partly dysfunctional family, there were lots of times in her teenage years that Esther felt awful. She hardly knew how she could go on living.

Why was she ever born if she was not loved?

She felt that she was always alone, so alone. It was hard to explain what that meant. Esther had a mother and a brother. They loved her, she knew that, but why had her father never shown her any love?

I love him but he hates me! She would cry to herself.

Esther would admonish herself - it sounded crazy! She had everything, a room of her own, good clothes, good food, and yet she felt so lonely. Without her father's love she felt dead inside!

Her parents had broken up many years ago but in her mind the day that her mother told her that her father would be leaving played out like a worn old movie.

She and Levi had been down by the lake playing and her mother, fighting back the tears, told her that even though Levi was still so small, her father would be leaving them. Esther felt as though she had been hit in the chest by a heavy weight. She ran home and went to her room where she cried for hours. Her whole world seemed to have been blown apart.

The realization that she was going to lose her father forever crept over her. It was so hard, even though she had hardly known him. She had probably only met him ten times. He was cold towards her as well, awkward, even though she loved him.

She kept asking herself, "What does God want from you, Esther?" Why does God let one suffer so much? He must see how much you hurt. Esther couldn't stand it much longer as she felt she was going to get sick. It was a terrible feeling.

At school, she broke down time and again and had to vomit. The nurse couldn't find anything wrong with her. But Esther knew what was wrong. She wanted to be loved, and she wanted to love. She tried so hard. She tried to love everybody, and she succeeded, even if a little. A lot of her friends, both boys and girls, used to come to her with their problems and would cry their hearts out on her shoulder.

When she was sixteen, Esther asked herself, "Doesn't God see you? Doesn't He look down upon you?" Esther began to think that God didn't love her anymore, that He, like her own father, would never love her. He had forsaken her.

Esther cried and cried and she asked many questions. She felt that the feelings boiling up inside her wiped everything out. Her youth was gone, and she would never be happy.

Now she blamed God, even though her heart was broken, and she was ashamed of her words.

Later she would ask for forgiveness; forgiveness from God the Almighty, whom she loved so much. But she thought in that desperate time that He was cold, just like her father when she told him, "I love you" and he just turned away.

Esther did not know what God wanted her to do and a deep wound would remain in her heart all through her life. It came from all the years when she felt she was alone, without him in her life.

Life throws all kinds of characters in our path as we grow up and some that stayed in Esther's mind were the acquaintances with annoying attitudes, those who were stingy and selfish, for instance.

Where men were concerned, it seemed to Esther as though she was a target for almost every man, all attempting to persuade her to have sexual relations with them, but Esther never succumbed. Rather, those experiences pushed her to be more hardworking, especially in her support of her mother. Esther drew up very clear boundaries with men, was very clear on what she would tolerate, reiterated what she would not, and by the Grace of God, she stuck with it.

She owed no one and understood that she had her own personal space, and that it was her prerogative to protect her space in the best way she could. Her boundaries clearly defined the kind of behaviors she could tolerate from men. If she had not been as realistic, she might well have been pushed over and misused sexually. Ignoring men was an effective method of pushing them away, back then. Ignored, they had no choice but to leave her alone, and find someone else.

As the end of childhood came and the beginning of womanhood beckoned, Esther knew that she had been deprived of a normal childhood. There had been no time in her childhood to visit places of interest, or have as much fun as other children. But Esther comforted herself that there would come a time where all pressure and difficulties would be behind her, when she would be able to enjoy all the good things she had missed previously. That time would come - when she got married.

Chapter Two

Moving Up and Getting On

Before Esther could entertain ideas of marriage, there was an academic mountain to climb. While her friends let boyfriends, clothes, boy bands and petty arguments on social media derail them, Esther kept her head down. She flew through her GCSE's and at 'A' level she did well and chose to study nursing. She had not been sure what she wanted to do while she was at school but she had done some volunteer work at a local hospice and had marvelled at the compassion and the dedication of the nurses who walked amongst the frailest patients who were preparing to relinquish their precious breath of life. The nurse's calm, cheerful and understanding ways visibly comforted the relatives of the patients there as well as in their homes.

Esther went with one of them on a home visit to a smart flat in a Mansion block. Inside, a man lay lifeless, his wife beside him dabbing water on his lips to keep his mouth moist. A carer called Brian hovered; ready to do the bidding of both the nurse and the wife while a daughter with a small dog sat sadly in the lounge. While the nurse talked to the carer, Esther sat next to the daughter, trying to offer what comfort she could. The man in the bed, surrounded by care and love, was clearly very close to death. But the arrival of the nurse seemed to lighten the mood and to throw a little light into the darkness. As the nurse stood beside the dying man, her hand on his and her smile reassuring, Esther realised that this was what she wanted to do - to bring quiet and calm and comfort in the darkest of places and during the hardest of times. Her love of God would be her compass that would guide her to be the best that she could be.

Esther worked hard and now that she had a goal she threw everything that she could into getting her qualifications.

She soon discovered that life as a student nurse meant that no two days were ever the same. There were clinical placements, presentations, lectures, and then there was simulated practice. It was a varied and challenging programme but Esther thrived on it.

She was studying for her Bachelor's degree in child and adult nursing. At the end of her first-year course, Esther was about to start a rotation in the neonatal unit. It was the start of her exciting nursing adventure and Esther was convinced she had made the right choice.

At home, her mother would hang on her every word fascinated by the stories of the tiny babies that Esther was helping to nurse.

"Small enough to fit in my hand you say?" She would ask wide-eyed and Esther would nod.

"Yes mum, tiny little babies, you would never think they could live, but the nurses and doctors are so skilled. When you first go in it is frightening, buzzers and alarms going off, but you get used to it."

Another placement for Esther was in the children's assessment unit, dealing with children, who had been referred by GPs, brought in by ambulance, or who community nurses had sent to the unit. The unit also offered open access for families with children who were suffering from longer-term conditions. Esther's heart broke for the little children with cystic fibrosis and spina bifida and other childhood-robbing conditions, their young bodies wracked with disease that would see no end. Mother's with care-worn faces brought in children who had seen too much suffering in their short lives. Where there should have been joy and laughter and play, quiet acceptance had taken over.

It was a 24/7 service unit with doctors and nurses working twelve-hour shifts that started at 7.30 am. Esther's day started with a briefing from the night team bringing the new shift up to date with the patients who were already in the unit. The mornings were hectic as the nurses assessed, treated and played with the children, talking and reassuring families and observed and gave out medication. The aim was to get as many of the children as possible to a stage where they could safely be discharged back home.

For any child not well enough to be discharged, arrangements had to be made for them to be admitted to either a surgical or a medical ward. Children who were seriously ill needed to be stabilised before they were transferred to a paediatric intensive care unit.

Working in the children's unit was hectic and often sad, but Esther thrived on the responsibility. Her kindness and gentle ways endeared her to families and children who were there with a full range of medical conditions. Esther learned that children tended to bounce back quite fast and as they did, their personalities would shine through.

Esther also went on a placement working in the community with a health visiting team and had the opportunity to study child development. She could not help thinking about her own development as a child, stifled by responsibility and worries that should never concern a child.

Esther was proving a very good nurse and her efforts did not go unnoticed. She was nominated for a place on a National Student Nurse Leadership Academy (NSNA) that had been a pilot project initiated to identify potential nurse leaders at an early stage. Esther attended a three-day course in Birmingham to discuss what change would mean in healthcare and how that change could be led. At the end of the course, the NSNLA students would return to their local areas to try and create improvements in their own working areas.

It was the first time that Esther had been away from home. As she arrived at the hotel that the course was to be held in, she examined the key that had been placed in her hand. Her, Esther, in a hotel room! The window of her room overlooked the busy street below and she looked around in wonder. There was a tea tray, a soft dressing gown and lots of small containers of shampoo and even slippers and a shower cap in the pristine bathroom. A bathroom all to herself!

As she walked towards the meeting room that the course was to be held in, she heard a voice beside her say:

"Lizzie Driffield, Lizzie Dripping to my friends!"

Esther laughed out loud and found herself face to face with a girl with flame red hair and freckles. She held her hand out and Esther noticed that even her hand had hundreds of freckles. Esther took it and said:

"Esther Washington, how do you do?"

"Woa! That's a bit formal isn't it mate?" Lizzie replied.

Esther felt herself blush. "Sorry I didn't mean ... I meant, ..."

Lizzie laughed.

"No worries Esther, I know you're a good un! " Lizzie put a slightly plump arm around Esther's shoulders and gave her a squeeze.

"Coming in?" Lizzie said. She indicated the door and the two girls walked in together.

The girls sat together and Esther felt the excitement rising within her. She knew that the opportunity she had been singled out for was a great one, and now it seemed she had someone to share it with. They had discovered they both lived in London, although Lizzie was originally from Liverpool.

Esther had made new friends at the university and at work and she had the feeling that she and Lizzie were going to be friends for a long time.

That evening, they met in the lobby before going out for something to eat. Going out in the evening was something that Esther never did. But she had brought money with her and the thought of actually eating in a restaurant was thrilling. Several of the other delegates were coming with them and one of them, a male nurse, seemed to be very interested in Lizzie. As they walked out along the streets, he slung his arm casually around Lizzie's shoulders, his hand trailing to just above her right breast. Esther glanced at her new friend, sure that she would be outraged, but Lizzie did not seem to mind at all. Maybe she knew him, Matt, his name was, maybe that was it. Esther thought.

As they sat down in an Indian restaurant, Esther sat next to Lizzie with Matt sitting on her other side. Esther noticed he had put his hand on her leg, a hand that seemed to be working its way upwards.

"Did you already know Matt?" Esther asked.

"Him? No, never met him before in my life! He's a cheeky one too!" Lizzie said half-heartedly, slapping his hand as it crept under the hem of her dress.

Esther tried to concentrate on her meal and ignore Matt and Lizzie who were almost on top of each other. Esther felt sad. She had been looking forward to the evening and getting to know Lizzie better but now it seemed that Lizzie was preoccupied with Matt. Esther did not drink but the others were drinking a lot. Esther knew that drinking tends to loosen the inhibitions and she never wanted to be in a position that she did not know what she was doing.

She tried to live her life by standards, it was all that she knew and her way had seen her make a success of her life until now. But she knew she was out of step with a lot of her peers who seemed to find getting drunk almost obligatory, every time they went out. Now she felt like an old-fashioned chaperone sitting stone cold sober while all around her, her companions were getting louder all the time.

By the time they went back to the hotel, it was obvious that Lizzie and Matt were going to be spending more time alone together and Esther headed straight to her room. She called her mother and told her about the events of the day. Though anxious about her being away alone from home, Esther's mother only became calm after endless reassurance from her.

"There is a great bunch of other nurses here, we have all just been out to eat!" She said. She did not mention to her mother anything about the drinking spree she had witnessed.

The next morning at breakfast, Lizzie appeared without Matt and made her way to where Esther sat.

"Oh my head," she said plonking herself down. "I need a coffee!"

Esther laughed. That was another advantage of not

drinking. She had slept well and was wide wake and feeling great, ready for the day.

"Matt not with you?" Esther ventured.

"No still snoring his head off. I wonder if we can get a discount 'cos his room wasn't used?" Lizzie gulped her coffee and smacked her lips. "That's better!"

Esther was stunned. While she had been expecting that her new friend had spent the night with Matt, actually knowing she had done so came as a shocker to her. The thought of sleeping with someone within hours of meeting them was so horrific that she could not imagine it. But then, she told herself, she was the unusual one. She knew that a lot of her school friends had been behaving like Lizzie for years. It didn't seem to mean anything to them. When Esther challenged one of her friends at school she shrugged and said:

"What's the biggie? It's just like shaking hands or sommat. It hurts the first time, a bit, but after that it's OK."

Esther was glad when Matt failed to turn up for breakfast giving her a chance to talk to Lizzie. Despite the fact that she did not agree or even understand what Lizzie had done, she liked her. She was a friendly girl and a confident one and she made Esther feel protected. As they were leaving, Matt appeared a rucksack over his shoulder.

"Hi, um...?"

"Lizzie!" Lizzie said patiently.

"Look I'm off, I'm not feeling well. Good luck. See ya."

"See ya." Lizzie said cheerfully, and linking arms with Esther, she steered them into the auditorium. At break and lunch they sat together again and when they set off for home they were on the same train back to London.

By the time they split up on the platform to go home they had exchanged phone numbers. Lizzie was due to start work at the same hospital that Esther was in soon but Esther had a feeling they would meet up before then.

At home, Esther's mother could barely contain her excitement. She was so proud of Esther and she let her know it daily. She asked for every detail of her daughter's trip and Esther obliged, telling her about Lizzie - but not everything about her new friend!

Esther's nursing degree was fifty percent time in clinical placement and fifty percent study at the university where she would take what she learned in the lecture hall into the wards. Over the following years of her study, her placement would be in various departments and wards and in different parts of the NHS so that she would be exposed to a full clinical experience. Once she was qualified, Esther would choose the area in which she wanted to specialise.

It was something that she thought about a lot. She was drawn to the children that she nursed and also towards any situation that needed patience and understanding. The rush and urgency of emergency medicine was not for her. Nor was ICU the place for her, where the patients were often unable to communicate. Her nature fit best as a quiet, comforting presence for those who need calm and a supportive presence the most.

Her time as a student nurse was an intense round of working shifts at nights and weekends and, when she was not nursing in the wards, there were essays to write as well as anatomy and pharmacology exams to prepare for. Despite being a hard worker, Esther still found the schedule exhausting at times. Talking to Lizzie was always a good diversion.

The two spoke often and Esther even managed to take a light-hearted view of some of Lizzie's more reckless behaviour because she liked her so much. It was great to talk about what was going on with study and work and Esther could not wait until Lizzie transferred to her hospital. The hospital was very close to Esther's home and she had tentatively suggested that Lizzie rent the room that her mother often let out to boarders, to save her from the hustle of travelling all across London. She was tentative because she knew that Lizzie's freewheeling lifestyle would not go down well with her mother at all.

Esther explained by saying:

"Mother is a bit, well, straight-laced, you wouldn't be able to have boys back or anything."

"Hey I'm off boys at the moment, too knackered!" Lizzie said. "Don't worry I'll behave myself! I hate this bedsit; it will be great to be back with a family. I kinda miss the old folks back in Liverpool!"

And it was settled.

The shifts and the way of work formed close communities of student nurses and for the first time in her life, Esther felt really part of something with others who all had a common goal to help others.

Esther found that she was drifting away from the friends that she had had in school. None of them had gone on to study and most now had one or more children and lived in council accommodation, most of them alone, the fathers of their children, like Esther's own father, long gone.

She would see them out and about pushing baby buggies and looking very far from the carefree girls she had known at school. It was not what Esther wanted for herself. Not remotely. She wanted to help people, she was going to get out in the world and make a difference, her faith was her guide and she was letting God take her where He wanted her to be.

Before she drifted off to sleep at night, Esther would often feel a moment of worry as she realised that in only five hours she would have to be back in the wards. She also had a recurrent thought that had nibbled at her consciousness for a while, a thought about being a lawyer. It was something very far removed from what she was doing, and she would have to admit that at this time there was nothing else she would rather be doing than study nursing. Working in healthcare was definitely relentless but she felt motivated by her patients and the other medical professionals that she came into contact with every day.

She had thought about studying law before she chose nursing but she did not feel ready for it, not confident enough or worldly enough to be in a world that was quite cutting edge and ruthless. The thoughts, however, never really left her and later in her life would come to the fore again. But that was a long way ahead of her now. For now Esther threw herself into her studies and into working with her patients. In what spare time she had, she worked at the hospice locally, the same one that she had volunteered in before her training, reading to the patients and sitting quietly with them.

One lady, an old woman, from Nigeria, was visited by a large family every day and smiled serenely at everyone while her life ebbed away. She lay with her hand on her Bible, a Bible that had seen many years of faithful service. Esther was reading from it when, with a final smile that lit up the room, the old lady died. Esther continued to read;

Yea, though I walk through the valley of the shadow of death, I will fear no evil: for thou *art* **with me; thy rod and thy staff they comfort me.** Thou *preparest a table before me in the presence of mine enemies: thou anointest my head with oil; my cup runneth over. Surely goodness and mercy shall follow me all the days of my life: and I will dwell in the house of the LORD forever.*

Chapter Three

Finding love and facing loss

Time passed in a whirl of work and study, the days merging into one for Esther. Before she knew it, Lizzie had moved in and was like a breath of fresh air in the house. Esther's mother loved her! She loved the way that Lizzie was always so bright and breezy and she loved the way that she seemed to bring Esther out of herself. At times Esther's mother, Ruth, worried that her daughter was working too hard, not taking enough time to herself. What she did not realise was that to Esther, her work was 'her time.'

After a childhood spent worrying about money and taking on too much responsibility, the end was in sight. The responsibility she was taking on was for her future, and she knew that the more work she put in the better her life would be. Esther still took time to go to church and to teach Sunday school but other than that, if she was at home, she had her head in a book.

It was about a month after Lizzie had moved in that Esther and her friend were both working in A&E. It was the least favourite of the rotations that Esther did but she was in the children's area helping out with the children, mostly with minor problems. The first little boy patient had pushed a little toy car up his nose. Esther's calming influence helped sooth him while the doctor fished it out.

Then there was a little girl having an asthma attack that was soon brought under control. Another little boy had fallen out of a tree and broken his arm and was proudly showing off his plaster cast. Suddenly, through all the noise and hubbub, the 'red phone' rang. Esther's heart always beat a little faster when the loud ring of that phone heralded the arrival of an emergency either by ambulance or air ambulance, usually a very serious case.

"Trauma call, male paediatric knife injury, five minutes." The sister called out and Esther felt her mouth go dry. She had been hoping desperately that it would be an adult trauma, she did not know if she was ready to see a child with a knife wound.

Immediately, the A&E department transformed into a battle-ready place with paediatricians and surgeons alongside the A&E consultants and specially trained trauma nurses, all going through well-practiced routines so that they would be ready when the casualty arrived. The sister who had been mentoring Esther told her to take care of the children waiting to be attended to in the waiting room.

Esther had not been trained in this kind of emergency situation and she was more than happy to help. A strange quiet descended on the department in the few moments before the doors burst open and a stretcher was wheeled through accompanied by an air ambulance doctor who was on top of the stretcher, his knees on either side of the motionless patient, pumping hard on his chest.

In seconds the lifeless body of the boy was transferred to a treatment couch and surrounded by professionals who connected him up to machines that would breathe for him and register every vital sign.

As Esther watched, a nurse took off the boy's trainers that were splattered with blood and put them to the side. Esther's heart suddenly stood still. Levi had trainers like that, just like that, they were his pride and joy and he never went out without them.

For a moment her legs would not move but suddenly she was lurching forward, vaguely aware of the shocked faces of the medical team as she pushed them to one side until she was standing over the boy. His face was covered with a breathing mask but there was no mistake. It was Levi.

"He's my brother," she croaked and then passed out.

When she came around, one of the air ambulance nurses was beside her and on the other side Lizzie stood, her face a picture of concern.

"Is he? Has he?" Esther asked.

"He's doing poorly but he is holding his own. Shall I tell you what happened on the way here?" The nurse asked her gently.

Esther nodded.

"Well, Levi had been drifting in and out of consciousness before he was flown here by air ambulance.

The A&E consultant who took over Levi's care from us says that his injuries are mainly to the liver and the liver usually heals itself, so I don't think they plan to operate. Once they know more the consultant will come and talk to you, I'm sure."

"Does my mother know?"

"Yes, I called her," Lizzie said.

"Oh well I better get up, I don't want her to have to worry about me too." Esther said.

"Are you sure?" Lizzie asked, as the air ambulance nurse said her goodbyes.

"I'm sure. I'm no use lying here. I need to find out what is going on with Levi. What on earth happened? Wasn't he at school?" Esther looked at her friend.

"It seems that he was bunking off school and somehow got into a situation in the park with a group of older boys. One of them had a knife and …" Lizzie tailed off.

As they looked over at the bay in which Levi was being treated they could see that he was about to be moved. The sister, seeing Esther hurried over to her.

"His blood pressure has dropped and we are sending him up to ICU." Before Esther could answer her mother was suddenly beside her, the colour drained from her face, her teeth chattering slightly with shock.

Esther and her mother clung together for a moment, but Levi's bed was being wheeled down the corridor now and they needed to follow it. Esther led her mother to the public lift and very soon they were standing outside ICU. The door was locked and they had to wait to be admitted.

When they were, Esther had to hold on to her mother to stop her from collapsing. It was a frightening sight. The patients were surrounded with machines that flashed and beeped and had readings tracing across them. In the corner Levi lay, his eyes closed and tubes leading from his mouth, his nose and into both arms. His covers were turned down to just at the top of his legs and a large dressing was visible over his abdomen.

Esther felt her mouth go dry again as she tried to take in what the registrar was telling them.

"His blood pressure is starting to recover now and as the damage is confined to his liver, we won't need to operate. I know that it looks frightening but Levi is young and strong and he will recover."

Esther looked down at her brother's face. He looked so young and she went cold when she thought that they could so easily have been in the morgue looking down at his lifeless body.

"Which department are you in?" The doctor asked, "I'm doctor Adam Ogenyemi, by the way."

"I'm a student nurse and I was in A&E when Levi was brought in, I'm Esther Washington and this is Levi's mother, Ruth." Esther indicated her mother who was staring at her son, her hand on his forearm so that she would not disturb the tubes that were snaking out from the back of his hand.

"Oh I see, that was rough, a real shock for you." The young doctor said frowning with concern, "But he is stable now and we are not expecting any setbacks."

"Thank you doctor," Esther's mother spoke now and Esther saw that tears were coursing down her cheeks. Her mother was a strong woman and Esther could not recall ever seeing her cry. She put her arm around her mother and with that she broke down and Ruth collapsed in her daughter's arms.

"I'll leave you for a moment." The doctor smiled kindly, and drew the curtain around the bed so that Ruth and Esther could be private with Levi.

By the end of the week, Levi was well enough to come home. Lizzie and Esther got a taxi to collect him. He was not the cocky youngster he had been before his injury and he seemed subdued and thoughtful. Esther thought that might not be a bad thing. She remembered a day when he was younger and both had passed a fight in the street.

There had been the flash of a knife, glinting in the sunshine and that had stayed with Esther. Levi had thought it was great excitement. "Cool." he said, as Esther dragged him away. She knew that the neighbourhood could be rough, and she worried for her younger brother's safety every day. He was always far bolder than her, more of a risk taker, and now he had paid the price for that.

It was some days after Levi had been discharged that Esther bumped into the young registrar again. She was sitting outside in warm autumn sunshine eating her lunch when he came and sat beside her.

"Esther, isn't it?" He smiled and Esther felt herself blush.

"Yes, doctor Ogenyemi?"

"Call me Adam, please!" He laughed, when people call me Dr Ogenyemi, I still think people are talking about my father!"

Esther laughed too. This young man had a knack of putting people at ease.

"You father is a doctor too?"

"Yes but he is in a teaching hospital back home in Lagos, Nigeria."

"My dad is Nigerian!" Esther said and then regretted it as Adam said.

"Oh? Is he in this country now?"

"I'm not sure," she said quietly. "I haven't seen him for a while."

"Say no more," Adam said, I guessed as much when he did not come to see Levi."

"Wow, do you remember all your patients so well?" Esther asked.

"Probably some not as much as others who have such beautiful sisters." Now Esther was blushing in earnest. As they ate, she looked sideways at Adam. He was tall and slim and very good-looking. But he had a softness to him, a kindness in his eyes that reminded her of something that her pastor had talked about in his sermon.

He had been talking to the young women of the congregation, and telling them what they needed to look for in their future husband.

Stop it Esther! She chided herself. She had only had a short conversation with Adam and already she was comparing him against the checklist that the pastor had talked about for a future life partner. What was *wrong* with her?

They talked for a bit longer about the hospital and about the rotations that Esther was on. She told Adam that she was drawn to the quieter side of medicine, the hospice work and working with chronically ill children.

"I'm impressed!" He said. "It's good that there are people like you who are prepared to step up in the less popular areas."

"I think that my faith helps." Esther said and watched him carefully for his response.

"Yes I can see it would, which church do you go to?"

"Manvers Street." Esther said.

"I go to St Peter's." Adam said and Esther felt something in her flutter like a butterfly stretching its wings.

Adam looked at his watch. "Better go, those patients won't heal themselves!" He quipped and Esther laughed again. "Maybe you would have a coffee with me sometime?" He said, and Esther nodded. She had never felt very comfortable in the presence of men; her mother's jaded view had made an impression on Esther. Her mother made no secret of her view that no man was to be trusted.

But for Esther, this stirring of romantic emotion was something that she had never felt before. She knew that for her there would be no question of any intimacy before she was married, and that, as far as she could see, would be a deal breaker for most young men. But somehow she knew instinctively that Adam was different. The timing was terrible, she needed to be concentrating on her studies, and really did not want to have any distraction, but that night as she lay in bed she could not help remembering the sermon her pastor had given that Sunday. He was quoting Dr Miles Monroe, a charismatic American preacher. It was he who had detailed the checklist that Esther had been thinking about so much and had said:

"A successful marriage has little to do with love, because love doesn't guarantee success. Love only brings happiness, but it doesn't bring what it takes to stay together. The only thing that makes marriage work is knowledge. You may love the person, but you need to know how to live with them. And that is where knowledge comes in. We are a Nation full of feelings and our insanity brings us to the altar. But you need to apply knowledge."

It was true, Esther thought as she lay staring at the ceiling, life is not all about love, it is about dealing with ups and downs, the pressures of life. After all, a diamond only becomes a diamond because of the extreme pressure it has been put under. Esther wished that Lizzie was not on night shift; she could really use her friends experience in matters of the heart.

Esther frowned. She was being ridiculous, "My goodness," she said out loud, "You only had one short conversation with him and half of that you had your mouth full of falafel sandwich!" But despite how she tried to justify it to herself, she could not deny the feelings she had. He was not the first man to have paid her attention, not by a very long way, and she had some friends who were boys, but none of them had ever made her feel the way that her brief encounters with Adam had made her feel.

After a sleepless night, as soon as she got to the hospital, Esther texted Lizzie who agreed to meet her for coffee at the end of her shift and before Esther's day shift started.

When she arrived in the hospital canteen, Lizzie looked tired. Esther had noticed that when her friend was tired she looked very pale and the freckles on her face would stand out more than ever. The girls hugged and Lizzie held Esther at arm's length.

"Now then, girlfriend," she said in a mock American accent, "What is with you? You look different."

Esther felt herself blush. It was no use trying to hide anything from Lizzie, it was like having a sister, and Esther loved her friend.

It came tumbling out, all the information, down to the last word of the conversation she had had with Adam with the quote from preacher Miles thrown in too!

"You've got it bad!" was all that Lizzie said when Esther came to a faltering halt.

"I have not!" Esther said indignantly.

"Oh come on! You look like you haven't slept a wink and you've dissected that muffin but not eaten a crumb of it! Those are two very good signs!"

Esther blushed deeper.

"Now look, I know that you have taken a vow of chastity and all that, but sister, let me tell you, that Dr Adam is a catch. He's a good man, a great doctor and he is so hot!" Lizzie looked at Esther, her eyes bright.

"I don't think of him like that!" Esther protested.

Lizzie cocked her head to one side and gave Esther a look that said that she did not believe her.

"Then you are made of stone young Esther, 'cos any red-blooded woman could see that he is a catch!" Lizzie said triumphantly. "I know how I can prove it. What was that checklist that you said your pastor said, the one that you can measure a man by, to see if he would make a good husband?"

"No one is talking about husbands!" Esther said.

"Ok, ok, just humour me though. How does it go?"

Esther shrugged.

"Number one he should be his own man, confident and comfortable in himself."

"Check!" Lizzie called out. "Two?"

"Number two, he should be a God-fearing man, a man who loves the Lord."

"Check! You said he went to church right?"

Esther nodded.

"Number three, he should work and be good at his work and have a purpose in life."

"Check and double check!" Lizzie said.

Esther smiled; her friend was so delighted with her exercise that, despite herself, Esther was getting into it now.

"OK number four he should cultivate his wife and make her the best she can be; he should be able to offer that kind of positive support."

"I'm going to say check!" Lizzie said. "It's obvious he would."

Esther smiled at her friend's logic.

"Go on!" Lizzie said.

"Number five," Esther said, "He should be able to protect her, and keep her safe."

Lizzie snorted, "Hell yeah! Of course he would!"

Esther laughed. Lizzie was so funny sometimes.

"The last one is that he should know God's word, know the bible and be able to take care of that side of life for his wife and children."

"Full house!" Lizzie threw her arms in the air in a triumphant gesture. "He goes to church, just like you, so of course he's up to speed with it all!"

Now Esther was laughing hard. Lizzie had a way of making things fit with her ideas but even so, Esther could not deny that from what she knew of him, doctor Adam Ogenyemi seemed to be a great example of someone who was perfect husband material.

She could not have known it in those early days but her relationship with Adam would last a lifetime, although not as she might have imagined. For now, the endless possibilities stretched before her and populated her dreams and thoughts. It was a gentle start to something that would be a constant anchor in her life.

Chapter Four
Possibilities beckon and wings are spread

Lizzie and Esther worked hard and finally, they graduated. They had worked together, laughed and cried together and helped each other along. They had encouraged each other, commiserated over bad marks and celebrated triumphs, they understood, and they explored new territories together, and finally, they graduated together, proud of their achievement and their friendship. They were more like sisters now.

As well as Levi and her mother, Adam came to see Esther graduate. As Esther watched from the podium, she saw her mother beaming at Adam. He was, since her father, the only man that had ever managed to get Ruth to let her guard down. But his quiet and gentlemanly ways and his obvious respect for her daughter had won her round and Adam was a frequent visitor for meals and for evenings at Esther's home.

Lizzie teased her friend mercilessly about the handsome young doctor. It was a very hard concept for her to grasp, the whole 'no sex before marriage deal', as she put it. But Adam knew that with Esther, that was non-negotiable and he seemed content with holding hands, and the kisses on the cheek and affectionate hugs that they shared, always being very careful not to overstep the mark.

Her graduation was Esther's proudest day and she was thrilled to have Lizzie and Adam as part of her 'family'. She had been so grateful for Adam's understanding while she was studying, that he had not pushed their relationship, that he had been steady and kind making sure that nothing he did distracted Esther from her studies.

Later, when everyone had left the house and the celebration and Lizzie had gone to see her parents off at the station; Adam and Esther sat alone in the lounge. Adam took her hand and kissed it.

"I am so proud of you Esther, you have worked so hard, you are going to be a brilliant nurse, a real credit to your mother."

Esther smiled. "Well, it was worth it, I can't wait to get started." For a moment, she rested her head on Adam's shoulder content to sit in silence, her hand in his. She felt his lips brush the top of her head and she closed her eyes. Now that she was relaxed with Adam, she felt unfamiliar stirrings and knew that she had to be careful. She knew that she could trust Adam, but could she trust herself? She knew that she loved this kind and gentle man. It reminded her of a saying: *Love is sweet, when you are with the right person.* Esther thought that she agreed with that, one hundred percent.

Esther was relaxed with Adam. She had at first been ready with her defences and that had made for a bit of awkwardness until she realised that Adam really would respect her boundaries and that she could be herself with him. He helped her with her studies, and although their shifts meant that they did not get to see each other as much as they would have liked, she felt happy knowing that he was her special friend.

As the weeks turned into months and then a year since their graduation, in the ward, Esther was with a young girl, Kayleigh, who had been injured in a fire. The thirteen-year old had horrific burns on her face and was inconsolable. Esther did her best to comfort her but the young girl's heart was breaking.

She was no longer in pain but the damage that the fire had done was too much for her to bear. Esther spent hours after her shift had finished and after Kayleigh's visitors had left trying to convince the girl that how she looked did not define her. But it was a difficult message to get through to a girl who was at the brink of teenage life where appearance was everything.

"I feel as though I have been locked in a cage, I'll be a freak for people to prod at with sticks!"

"You will not be Kayleigh, not at all. Haven't you got a good heart?"

"Yes," the girl said quietly.

"Don't you look after your little brother and sister wonderfully for you mum?"

"Yes." Kayleigh said.

"Don't your friends love being with you because you have a laugh together?"

"'S'pose." Kayleigh sniffed.

"And does what you look like affect any of those things?" Kayleigh shrugged.

"You know Kayleigh, I have a very special person in my life, the Lord Jesus, and he helps me through everything that happens to me. You think that you are going to be locked in a cage because of your scars. Well, the scars will fade and *there has never been a lock manufactured that did not have a key. Similarly, God never gives problems without solutions. We just need patience to unlock them.*"

"But just look at me!" Kayleigh wailed.

"When did you have your accident?" Esther asked quietly.

"Two weeks ago." Kayleigh sniffed.

"And does your face look better than it did then?"

"Yes, a bit."

"And as time goes on it will look better still." Esther said.

The young girl held Esther's hand tight and for the first time a small smile played around her lips.

"Do you really think so?"

"Well, you've seen the improvement in just two weeks, with your own eyes. And you know how clever the doctors are here."

Kayleigh nodded and the smile got a little bigger.

"Thank you nurse." She said. "When I finish school I'm going to be a nurse just like you!"

Esther was delighted. To know that the little girl was thinking ahead and not just feeling that her life was over was a huge bonus and she said a little prayer of thanks.

Kayleigh would never forget the nurse who had sat with her in her darkest hour and showed her that she did have a future.

It was one evening not long before Christmas that Lizzie breezed into the house, her excitement bubbling out of her. Esther had just said good night to Adam and was about to go to bed.

"Oh no you don't," Lizzie grabbed Esther by the hand and pulled her down the stairs and back into the lounge.

"Look at this!" She waved a flyer in the air.

"How can I look at it if you are waving it about?" Esther laughed, "What is it?"

"This, my dear, is your ticket to freedom and fortune!" Now Esther was intrigued and tried to snatch the paper out of Lizzie's hand but her friend skipped neatly out of her way and held the paper up high so that even jumping up, Esther could not reach it. Finally, the girls collapsed onto the settee and Lizzie relinquished the paper to Esther with a flourish.

Esther started to read:

Nurses wanted for Saudi Arabia

Our client is a unique prestigious Health Care provider with a focus on providing 24-hour and seven days a week cover for any medical and nursing care required by the Royal Family and Military personnel in Riyadh, Kingdom of Saudi Arabia. The Hospital is fully equipped with all medical and surgical departments such as: Ophthalmology and ENT rooms, Trauma room, a V.I.P. ICU Suite, Paediatric examination facilities, X-ray and Physiotherapy treatment rooms, Dermatology treatment rooms, Oncology, Psychiatry, Endocrinology and Orthopaedics, a Pharmacy, Dental treatment rooms and Protocol and Medical Records offices.

The client also has a location in Jeddah that is staffed throughout the year and staff generally transfer to this location for 4-6 months a year. In order to keep nursing knowledge fully up to date, each Nurse will be on a clinical rotation (on an annual basis) with one of the biggest hospitals in the Kingdom (King Faisal Specialist Hospital & Research Centre in Riyadh).

Job description:
Direct Reporting to: Immediate Charge Nurse/Supervisor
Job Title: Various Nursing

Purpose of Job:
To provide acute patient care by utilizing specialized nursing skills and knowledge under the supervision of senior medical staff, in line with policies and procedures set by the client.

Requirements:
- *Bachelor Degree in Nursing and experience in well-known institutes*
- *Excellent level of English*

Mental/Emotional Requirements:
Ability to:
- *Handle multiple priorities*
- *Make decisions under pressure*
- *Manage stress appropriately*
- *Work alone effectively*
- *Work in close proximity to others and/or in a distracting environment*
- *Work with others effectively*

Key Accountabilities & Activities:
Patient Care
- *Provide acute care to patients in order to stabilise them*
- *Obtain samples/vital signs/blood samples and coordinate with laboratory and radiology team to process fluid samples and medical images in order to provide attending doctors accurate status of patient's health condition*
- *Undertake interventions within, such as resuscitation, defibrillation, IV Cannulation etc. in order to provide acute care to patients*
- *Accompany patients during medical evacuations and transfers in order to facilitate medically safe patient transfer*

- *Adhere to quality and safety standards in operations and aim to ensure an infection-free environment*
- *Retrieve patient medical history and maintain medical records taking into consideration confidentiality as per policy and procedures of the client*
- *Participate/attend skills maintenance programs of the unit in order to keep skills current and stay abreast of latest developments in the nursing field.*

Policies & Procedures
- *Follow all relevant policies, processes, standard operating procedures and instructions so that all work is carried out in a controlled and consistent manner*
- *Contribute to the identification of opportunities for continuous improvement of systems, processes and practices taking into account leading practices, profess efficiency, cost reduction and productivity improvement*
- *Promote the implementation and adherence to policies, processes and operating procedures to others within the clinic*
- *Maintain confidentiality of all information and ensure treatment-related details are handled in accordance with policies and procedures of the client*

Benefits:
- *Attractive salary depending on experience (starting at approximately 20,000 SAR per month)*
- *Free housing accommodation/housing allowance is provided to expatriate employees**
- *Free twenty-four hours transportation services provided from housing accommodation to hospital and vice versa*
- *Daily scheduled shopping trips for employees living in single female accommodation*
- *One annual ticket for a round trip air ticket for employees*
- *Annual merit increase*
- *Repatriation Air Ticket provided*
- *The Clinic will provide all eligible employees with Medical Insurance*

- *Free Medical Primary Care including (Radiology services, dental, medication etc.)*
- *End of Services Award Bonus*

As she got to the part about the salary, Esther asked her friend, "How much is 20,000 riyals in pounds?"

"Don't you worry sister, I've already checked on that. It's – wait for it – four thousand and forty-eight pounds and, count 'em, 74 pence – oh yeah! And for you ma'am, that is completely free of tax!" Lizzie finished with a bow.

"Wow" Esther said quietly, reading the document through again. "And you really think they would take us?"

"Hell yeah! They will be lucky to have us and have you read all about the benefits, the air tickets, the leave, the bonus?" Lizzie was breathless with excitement.

"I need time to take it in Lizzie, but it really is very exciting. No tax? That will make it easy to save a lot of money fast, I could send money home for mum so that she can slow down with the work a bit."

Lizzie nodded eagerly. She could see that she was winning her friend around.

"It's late, I've got to go to bed, let's talk about it tomorrow?" Esther said.

Lizzie gave her a hug. "Ok nighty, night but I know this is the right thing for us, and we will have each other to go with, which is more than most other nurses have!"

Esther did not sleep much that night. She kept putting on her bedside light and reading the advert again, until she knew it by heart. She was in turmoil. The thought of going abroad was daunting when until now she had only left home once, for a night, to go to Birmingham! But the idea was also exciting. The chance to travel to meet other people in different cultures and to earn money that would, at last, allow her mother to take it easy, was overwhelmingly tempting. But could she do it? And what about Adam?

Lizzie was still asleep when Esther woke up to prepare for work. By the time Esther was leaving for the hospital the next morning, her mind was still full of the thought of applying for the nursing job in Saudi Arabia. She thought about Adam again. They had been seeing each other for over a year now and they were no further forward.

Esther realised that 'further forward' for most couples would mean taking their relationship to a physical level, but Adam knew that Esther would not do that, and so they remained the most benign of boyfriend and girlfriend with occasional hand-holding and chaste kisses, mostly on the cheek, being all the physical manifestation that they had to show for their seeming devotion to each other.

Esther chided herself. She had made it clear to Adam that she would not entertain intimacy before marriage but for some contrary reason, she worried that he did not try to take things further with her. Did he not find her attractive? Did he not have any desire for her? He showed no sign that he wanted to ask her to marry him either, maybe she thought, without physical contact a couple should not commit, what if that side of things didn't work? Could it not work?

Esther rubbed her temples; she was so confused. A little voice in the back of her head was telling her that she needed to think about her future for herself and not let Adam influence her decisions. As she got ready to take the medicine around to the patients on her ward, she decided that she would be able to tell what Adam's intentions and feelings were once she told him of the plan that Lizzie had to take them to the other side of the world.

At lunchtime she met Adam in the canteen. He was smiling as she walked over to his table with her tray.

"Hello there you globetrotter!" He said cheerily, "Have nursing degree will travel?"

"You heard?"

"Lizzie." They said together.

"Yes, I called this morning and she answered." Adam smiled, "It sounds really exciting, tell me all about it."

Well, Esther thought to herself; clearly Adam was far from distraught that she might be leaving. Esther began to tell him the details; she had read the leaflet so often that she almost knew it by heart. When she came to the part about the salary, Adam gave a low whistle.

"Wow, that is more than I get! It sounds like a no brainer to me! How long till you leave?"

Esther looked at Adam's eyes, bright with enthusiasm for her and the idea of a new career in the Middle East and she could not help feeling a bit sad that he almost seemed to be in a hurry to get rid of her. But one good thing was that it made her mind up for her. She would tell Lizzie as soon as she saw her - she was in!

With whirlwind Lizzie behind the great Saudi escape, things moved pretty fast. Visas were obtained, medicals completed and notice given at the hospital. There had been a going away party for the girls a couple of nights before and Adam, far from appearing to be sad, seemed as excited as Esther was. Esther did not know what to make of it. And now she was sitting on the edge of her bed, her last minute packing done ready for her last night at home.

Adam would be picking them up to take them to the airport in the morning. Suddenly there was a tap and Levis face appeared around the door. He was ready for bed too, wearing only pyjama bottoms and Esther winced as she saw the scar that had been left by her brother's knife attack.

"Well sis, I really just came in to see if I could have your room?" He said with his lopsided smile.

"No you can't! I'm not going forever!" Esther laughed.

"I hope you aren't," Levi said, his smile slipping, "I'm gonna miss you." And suddenly he was a little boy again, his eyes filled with tears. Esther hugged him.

"I promise I'll be back. I get my first leave after 6 months, and then I'll be home. The time will go really fast."

Levi smiled at her. "You gonna write to me?"

"You gonna write back?" Esther laughed.

"I'll send you an email every day if you want me to." She added.

"Steady on sis, I can't write back that much!" And they laughed together.

Finally, the day came. Lizzie had gone to spend the last week with her family in Liverpool so she and Esther would be meeting up at terminal three, Heathrow. Levi and her mother came with Adam and Esther to the terminal. It was an awkward journey with Esther's throat aching as she tried to hold back the tears and her mother staring out of the window, possibly trying to hide her own tears.

Even Levi was quiet until they got close and he started to see the huge airliners stacked in the clear blue sky above the airport, waiting for their slots to land. Esther swallowed hard. This was it. She was about to fly thousands of miles away from home.

Adam was talking about parking the car now but Esther put her hand on his arm. "Don't park Adam please, just drop me off, I really don't think I can handle a long goodbye." To Esther's huge relief, Adam nodded in understanding and pulled up at the drop off point near the terminal.

They said their goodbyes outside one of the busiest airports in the world, where the noise of planes and people drowned their sobs. And then her mother, Levi and Adam were gone and Esther was left to make her way into the terminal to find Lizzie and then travel on to a new life, six thousand miles away.

Chapter Five
A new challenge and a new decision

As they stepped off the plane and felt a blanket of heat hit them in the face, they made their way to the baggage collection area at the huge and futuristic looking King Khaled Airport in Riyadh. Esther knew immediately that her life was going to change in a very profound way.

Giggling, she and Lizzie had put on their abayas, the long silky coverall that came down to the ground and covered their arms, in the plane's washroom but as they looked around in the arrivals lounge, their plain black abayas set them apart from the Muslim women who were mostly veiled from head to toe. The sight of these women completely covered in black looked strange and slightly shocking. To Esther, it also felt unsettling. She and Lizzie could not have known how soon this article of clothing would become something that they threw on automatically, every time they went out.

Their accommodation was in a place called Iskan, the Arabic for home, where their en suite rooms overlooked a central pool and a guard on the gate controlled who came and went and one thing you knew for certain was that they would never include the male of the species in this all-female compound. Each floor had a shared kitchen but most people seemed to eat in the hospital canteen that was heavily subsidised and segregated into male and female eating sections.

The first week of Lizzie and Esther's time at the Riyadh Military Hospital was a busy time. Each morning, Esther and Lizzie would meet outside their accommodation block and catch the shuttle bus that took them to the huge hospital campus and the main body of the hospital. It was January, and as the sun rose, they marvelled at the fact that although it was a nippy +6C at 7:30 am, by mid-day it would be over 20C.

That would not last for long, they knew. Riyadh is in the middle of the desert and although temperatures could drop at night in the winter, and be pleasant during the day, in the summer the heat would be punishing, day and night.

Their first days were hectic. The girls made their way to the post-graduate centre for a host of lectures, classes and introductory presentations aimed at introducing them to the various hospital departments. They had ID numbers issued, and were measured for their uniforms that would be tailored to fit them, and they had bank accounts opened so that they could transfer money home.

After a week of introductory activities, it was time to start their individual work experiences in the respective departments in which they had been hired to work. Lizzie was to work in A&E and Esther report to paediatrics.

There was a lot to take in for Esther. Not only was she in a new country coping with more than one foreign language, culture and religious ideology, (a lot of the nursing staff were from The Philippines.), in her new workplace, even the most commonplace pieces of nursing equipment were packaged differently than she was used to. Trying to keep calm, her eyes scoured the supply shelves looking for 4x4's and IV tubing. Even the pieces of equipment that she had been using every day in London and could describe with ease, were packaged differently here. It was disconcerting

Esther found herself the only person in a staff of 25 on the ward whose native language was English. It was true that English was the working language of the hospital, but every single person she worked with had some kind of accent. It was a wonderful mix of Middle Eastern, Filipino, Malaysian and Indian dialects with the head nurse being from the Netherlands and another Turkish nurse who had started at the same time as Esther. In the ward, although not in the hospital, Esther was the only nurse from England.

Even something as simple as answering the phone turned out to be a challenge. Although Esther knew the caller on the other end of the line was speaking in English, often, she could not understand a single word they said. Doctors used their first names, and there were some names that seemed to be very popular. "Dr Rashid" was one of a dozen or more in this hospital, but he would expect whoever answered the phone to be able to identify him! Esther often found herself confused between which were male and which were female Arabic names and as well as that it was not uncommon to have two patients with the same names.

Esther quickly learned the best way to identify her patients was by their medical record number when she had to have clinical discussions about them.

As she gradually got used to her new way of life, Esther felt that every aspect of her life, the physical, emotional and spiritual being were being stimulated and challenged at the same time. She always wanted to be open-minded, and really tried hard never to be judgmental. She wanted to take advantage of new opportunities.

At the Riyadh Military Hospital, there was immense latitude for one to expand his/her expand professional scope. In a country where money was no object, there was cutting-edge everything and things like CT scans and MRI's that would incur a long wait in the UK, were done as a matter of routine with several of the machines in each hospital.

Esther and Lizzie had found themselves with very little time between their shifts and settling in but one thing that they did agree on was that although they had felt very confident with their nursing skill-sets when they arrived, they had both developed an added respect for the nurses they were now working with, from both a technical and an efficiency point of view.

The Riyadh Al Kharj Hospital was mainly for the treatment of military personal although it did have a VIP wing in South West Corner, a newly built part of the hospital, one floor below the paediatric ward that was Esther's work station. Sometimes she would see the kerfuffle when someone from the very large Royal family was being taken up in the lift that went directly to the VIP suite.

Once one of the young doctors, a distant member of the Royal family himself, took her up there when the wing was empty. Esther was dumbstruck. Everywhere was decorated in the most opulent furnishing and with what she realised was real gold. All the bathrooms had gold taps, and only the hospital beds in the patient rooms gave any clue that this was a hospital and not a luxury hotel.

Lizzie had been sent to a satellite hospital to work for a couple of weeks and Esther missed her. The hospital site had an indoor swimming pool and tennis courts, and as the weather was very cool in the evenings, she enjoyed the chance to learn to play tennis and to swim in a pool that was for women only.

While Lizzie was away in Al Kharj, Esther was transferred to Oncology. It was a shock for her. Unlike the UK, cancer education was almost non-existent in The Kingdom and as a result, the patients came with much later stage disease. Most of them were beyond treatment. All the doctors and nurses could do was to keep them comfortable. It was sad, but Esther had to steel herself to try and comfort her patients.

Towards the end of the clinic one afternoon, there was a commotion out in the waiting area. Esther ducked out of the consulting room and was shocked to see a young Filipino woman being escorted by two prison guards, her feet and hands manacled.

The other patients waiting for the clinic were staring openly at the terrified young woman and Esther hurried her into an empty clinic room. When she told the registrar about the patient, he told Esther that the young woman, who was called Malaya had come for test results that showed that she had breast cancer.

"The problem is, the prison is not likely to let her come in for treatment." The doctor told Esther. He was a young Saudi called Hesham and he always made it very plain that he liked working with Esther.

Esther was horrified. "But she is so young! That can't be allowed!"

Dr Hesham shrugged.

"Unfortunately Filipinos in this country are considered as menials, servants with virtually no rights and no one prepared to fight for them." The doctor looked at Esther speculatively. She was obviously passionate.

"The problem is that I cannot go to the prison to plead her case. Only women can go there."

"I'll go!" Esther said without hesitation.

The doctor smiled at her. "That's marvellous, let's go and see the patient, nurse."

The patient, Malaya, was terrified. Esther could hardly bear to look at her haunted face, etched with worry and sorrow.

As Esther moved towards the terrified woman, who stood, just skin and bone in her prison uniform barefoot and shaking, the guards pushed her away. Esther could not even touch the woman.

Esther was nearly moved to tears. She closed her eyes for a moment and thought about an inspirational saying that she hoped would give her strength.

Life can be full of unexpected things, either happy or sad but no matter what happens just keep a loving heart and a wise mind and a strong faith in God. He will always stay with us, through all our life's journey.

The doctor was talking to the guards, obviously imploring them to allow the woman to come for treatment. But the guards were not the decision-makers and just shrugged. The doctor sent Esther up to the medical secretaries with a tape that contained a letter he would send back to the prison. The letter detailed the treatment that the young woman needed, starting with a mastectomy and then going on to radiotherapy. He hoped at this stage that chemotherapy might not be needed if the surgery and radiotherapy could be given right away.

Esther took the guards and the young prisoner to a side room to wait for the letter and then asked one of the Fillipino nurses, called Baby to wait with them. Maybe she could speak to the young woman in her own language and give her some comfort. Thinking fast, Esther gave the nurse a form. "Pretend to be taking some details, otherwise I don't think that her guards will let you speak to her." Baby nodded.

Esther liked Baby. The nurse had explained that the last child of a Filipino family was often called Baby and she told her that Malaya, the name of the young woman prisoner, meant 'free' in her language. The two nurses exchanged glances as he considered the irony and Baby went into the room to talk to Malaya, pretending that she was filling in a form.

Once the letter was ready, the young Filipino woman was led away, her chains clanking and people staring. Esther saw tears of humiliation and fear rolling down the face of the poor woman and her heart broke.

At break, she and Baby went for coffee and Baby told Esther the woman's story.

"Apparently she was working for a Saudi family. The husband was using her for sex and the wife found out. To get her out of the house she claimed that Malaya had stolen money." Baby shook her head. "It's a story common enough. Often, the girls who come here to work in private houses are little more than slaves.

Some families are kind and good and fair but others take their passports away and never get them the exit visa they need to go home. Sadly, our embassy will rarely get involved. Despite the risks, many girls want to come here and earn money. Things are hard at home, and mothers are prepared to come and leave children in the hope of earning money to give them a better life. Some of them never return."

Esther was shocked and more determined than ever to do what she could to help the poor patient.

The arrangement for her to visit the prison seemed to take ages and Esther was conscious all the time that the Filipino girl needed to be operated on as soon as possible. Then finally the day arrived and Esther was outside the very forbidding prison located in a part of the city that she had never visited before. The smell hit her first, it was awful and she could hear the noise of the inmates, some wailing and crying and others shouting in the general hubbub.

Esther felt afraid, she was out of her depth. As she waited for the huge gates to be opened with several keys in several locks, she closed her eyes for a moment and a saying that had often sustained her came to her mind.

"Sometimes you might think you are being buried when you are actually being planted, God is using this season to grow you."

Esther immediately felt better, stronger and ready to take on the challenge that God was giving her. She soon realised that she certainly needed that strength when she got inside the prison. It stank. It was hot without air conditioner and the women seemed to be held in large cells, accommodating about twenty, with thin mats on the ground to sleep on.

Many of the women were Filipino and as she walked past the long row of cells the woman that Esther had come to plead for ran to the bars and put her very thin arm out. Her eyes were haunted and her expression the picture of despair. Esther held out her hand noticing how big it was compared to the arms poking out through the bars. Esther was a slim girl but next to most of these malnourished women she looked huge.

The guards were quick to react to this contact and viciously hit at the Filipino woman's arm. Malaya withdrew her arm and yelped in pain. The guards pushed Esther forward before she could say anything, but the indignation of the treatment Malaya had received burned her. Inside, Esther felt anger and an overpowering feeling of injustice. There was no one human enough to help these women; they were like dogs in a dog pound desperate to catch the eye of someone who could help them. Esther fought back the tears. Something new stirred inside her, a feeling that needed to be explored, but for now she needed to concentrate on helping Malaya.

The governor of the prison was a stern and sour-faced Saudi in full traditional dress. He took the medical reports that Esther had brought and, leaving her standing in front of his desk flanked by the two women guards, took his time to read the reports, answering his phone twice and having long conversations with the callers, while Esther stood, her legs almost giving way beneath her, as the heat overwhelmed her.

Coffee was served to the governor and he took his time to drink it, and to eat some fruit before resuming his scrutiny of the medical report Esther had brought. Finally, some forty-five minutes after she had been shown into the governor's office, Esther had her answer. Malaya was to return to the hospital with her and be admitted for surgery. Esther almost fainted with relief. As she was led back through the corridors alongside the cells, she saw Malaya again and smiled at her broadly. The Filipino woman understood the message and dissolved in tears.

Outside in the transport that the hospital had laid on for her, Esther gulped in the air-conditioned air. She felt elated that the woman would be able to have the surgery she needed to save her life.

A single guard came out with Malaya and still in her leg and wrist chains the Filipino girl was bundled into the back of the car between Esther and the guard. The smell emanating from Malaya was almost overwhelming - she had clearly not washed in many days if not weeks. But Esther took her hand nevertheless, and Malaya smiled at her with gratitude in her eyes.

Under her breath Esther recited an inspirational saying she had read.

"Believe in yourself, even when no one else does"

She knew that Malaya understood a little English and she hoped that she would understand what Esther was trying to say, and as the young woman's face lit up with a smile that showed that, without the pain, she was a beauty, Esther knew that she did understand.

That night with Malaya washed and safely in a single room on the ward, Esther went wearily back to her room, catching the last shuttle bus. As she lay in bed exhausted but still too full of the day's events to sleep, she explored the feeling that she had had at the prison, the feeling that had begun as a little seed when she saw the desperate faces of the women in prison and that was now becoming a plant growing in her heart and soul. It took her back to the time that she had wanted to be a lawyer, and had abandoned the idea partly because unlike nursing, there was no help with the fees, and she had also felt she was too naïve.

Now, however, she knew without any doubt what her future had to be. She had been sent to this desert land for a reason. As she prayed, the vision of her future became clear to her. She would work hard in Saudi Arabia for the money to fund her training in law, once she got back to the UK. And then she would take that training and concentrate on human rights law in combination with international corporate governance and financial law, she would do what she could to help women like Malaya. As she finished her prayers, a sense of peace descended on her and she fell into deep sleep. God had shown Esther her future.

Chapter Six

New love and old love and a friend in trouble

Malaya's surgery went well and as Esther stood with Dr Hesham at the end of her bed examining her chart, they felt a sense of relief. She was doing well and now they were waiting for the pathology to come back. That and the surgeons report confirming that the margins around the tumour were clear meant that Malaya would have a good chance. Once she had recovered, she would have radiotherapy.

Normally a patient would go home to recuperate and then come as an outpatient for the radiotherapy but in Malaya's case Dr Hesham was determined to keep her on the ward. She was badly malnourished and the last place she needed to be was back in the filthy prison. He and Esther knew that if she did go back it was very unlikely she would be allowed to return to the hospital for the radiotherapy treatment she needed.

Esther visited the young Filipino woman often, bringing Baby with her so that they could speak more than Malaya's limited English would allow. Esther learned that she had left her two young children behind, under the care of her mother. She had been in the Kingdom for three years, working up to 18 hours a day, with no time off, and no pay until she had been sent to prison 6 months ago.

She had been told that she would get a ticket to travel home once a year, but any enquiry she made of her employer was met with brusque dismissal. Her employer, a government minister, had started to rape her, coming into her room late at night when the rest of the house was asleep, often drunk and always rough. Drink was strictly prohibited in this strict Muslim country but was readily available to those who could pay for it.

Esther's heart broke for Malaya and for all the other women, and men who had no one to fight their corner. She had no idea how she was going to do it, but somehow she was going to get Malaya back home to the Philippines. The guards from the prison had stopped coming now, and that gave Esther hope.

When Lizzie came back from her trip, she came with Esther to visit Malaya. She felt sorry for the Filipino girl but she was worried for her friend too.

"Esther you need to be very careful, this is not the UK, you could just as easily take Malaya's place in prison if you overstep the mark."

"I know, I am being careful but I simply cannot turn my back on her."

Lizzie hugged her friend. She knew that it would be impossible to talk her friend out of what she was doing, but she also knew how dangerous it would be to get on the wrong side of the law in Saudi Arabia.

Malaya occupied Esther's thoughts a great deal of the time. She felt depressed at times because she thought she would never find a way to help her. At her darkest times she thought of a saying that had always helped her when she felt down.

'Don't dwell in negativity and stress, take a step back, gather yourself and pray. Fight through it and focus. Have a positive mindset.'

Esther prayed a lot and one sweltering day in June, her prayers were answered. A minor member of the Saudi Royal family, along with his wife brought their maid in to be seen by Dr Hesham. The concern of the couple was obvious and for their plump and obviously cared for and loved Filipino maid, this was clearly the very opposite of the circumstances in which Malaya had found herself.

As the prince's wife and Dr Hesham went into the examination room, Esther tried to reassure the prince. Before she knew it, the maid being comforted by the princess had come out of the room. The young Filipino needed to be admitted and operated on for what was thought to be cervical cancer.

Esther's mind was whirring. She would see if the ward would put the two young women in the same room as company for each other.

The ward agreed and over the next few weeks the two Filipinos became good friends. As she knew they would be, the Prince and his wife were touched by Malaya's story and had arranged for her to return to the Philippines after her treatment. But more than that they had also offered her a job with them, when she had recovered. Esther gave thanks to God every day for the way he had taken the problem from her and solved it. Malaya was going to be fine.

Esther's experience with Malaya had made her even more determined that when she got back from Saudi she would train in law. She was not sure of the exact course she could do; she would find that out when she returned to the UK on leave. When she told Lizzie of her plans, her friend was shocked.

"But Esther you're such a good nurse, surely that's a better thing to do than to shuffle around dusty old law books?"

"But the area that I want to specialise in will help lots of people, people who have no one else to fight for them, people like Malaya."

Lizzie shrugged. She knew that Esther was a very determined person. She might be quiet and naive but she knew what she wanted and this was clearly something that she had decided on and would not budge.

"Well I hope you're not planning to shoot off anytime soon?" Lizzie said.

"No, I have a lot of money to save first!" Esther said.

Lizzie and Esther had been in Saudi for two years now and their first contract was coming to an end. Both had been offered extensions and Esther was calculating if she had enough money to start her studies. She had been home only once and where other girls had taken their leave to visit exotic places, Esther had not, saving as much as she could, while sending money home regularly to her mother and Levi.

It was winter again in the Kingdom and Esther was sitting outside in the gardens of the hospital when she heard a voice.

"Penny for your thoughts?" It was Dr Hesham.
"Isn't that what you say in your country?"
Esther laughed, "It is! Where did you learn that?"

"I did my medical degree in the UK," Dr Hesham said. "By the way, you did a great job with Malaya. I heard from her Saudi sponsor family, she's back with them now, healthy and full of gratitude for your help."

Esther hesitated. She wanted to tell the young doctor about her plans, but what would he think? So far she had only spoken to Lizzie about it.

"Something on your mind?"

Esther looked at him, and decided she would tell him. Dr Hesham listened carefully to what she was saying. When she was finished he said,

"I think it is clear what your path should be. You are an excellent nurse and I would be very sorry to see you leave nursing and especially sad to see you leave the Kingdom, but I know what it is to have a vocation, a vision for your future, and you clearly have one."

"I do," Esther said firmly.

"How soon do you think you might be leaving?"

"Well my contract is up soon and I am just working out if I can afford to go back now or if I need to stay longer to get the money I need together."

"I really will be sorry to see you go." He said again and this time as his eyes met Esther's she saw something that went beyond a professional interest, a long way beyond.

Esther was taken aback. She knew that in the Kingdom it was strictly forbidden for an unmarried woman to be alone with a man who was not her husband or male relative although that obviously did not apply in a medical setting. The penalty for men and women who were not married being caught together, in the most extreme cases, was death.

Esther realised that she had ignored the signs that had all been there. It was the same look that Adam had to begin with, the one that had filled her own heart with flutter and excitement. Hesham had feelings for her.

Confused and alarmed, Esther jumped up from the bench and muttering her apologies she bolted for the safety of the ward. But that was not going to be the end of it, that night as she returned to the nurses' station, Dr Hesham was standing reading a patient's notes. There was no one else around and as she got to the station he said,

"I am very sorry about earlier." He said, his dark eyes looking at her with great concern.

"I just could not hide my feelings anymore." He moved around the desk until he was standing in front of her. His aftershave assaulted her senses and despite her self-restraint, Esther felt herself lean in towards him. Before she knew it, their lips had touched. Immediately they sprung apart, as if they had been stung. Anyone could have appeared at any minute. Esther felt as though her legs might give way and Hesham looked shocked, he had put them both at risk, and he was mortified.

"I am so sorry, forgive me," he spluttered and grabbing some files almost ran off the ward. Esther sat down heavily on a chair. Her heart was racing and her mouth was dry. She was confused. Very confused.

When she told Lizzie what had happened, her friend gave a low whistle.

"Living dangerously babe, living dangerously!" She said.

"I was not living dangerously, at least not on purpose. It just happened. I don't know what came over me."

"I don't know what came over you, although I have to say that Dr Hesham is one hot doc."

"Lizzie!" Esther felt herself blush.

"Well when it happens there is nothing you can do about it; trust me I know!" Lizzie said.

"When what happens?" Esther said warily.

"When you get the hots for someone!" Lizzie said.

"I did not get 'the hots' for Dr Hesham as you so crudely say."

"Look, you don't even know what 'the hots is' you are such a baby but you definitely got them, you have to trust me on this."

Esther was silent. As she tried to get some sleep ready for her next shift her mind was racing. What on earth was going to happen next?

What did happen next was something that Esther could never have imagined. As she crossed the huge hospital complex on her way to the ward, she heard a voice call her name. For a moment her mind struggled to identify the voice. It was familiar and her thoughts immediately went to Dr Hesham. As she turned around she came face to face not with Dr Hesham, but with Adam!

Esther was speechless. As Adam came towards her his arms outstretched to give her a hug she backed away.

"Adam no, you can't, it's not allowed!" Esther gasped.

"Oh yes, I forgot!" He said, putting his hand out to shake hers. Esther was not even sure that was OK but it felt very good to feel his hand in hers again. Esther felt as though she was going to burst into tears and for a moment they just stared at each other.

In Adam's eyes Esther could see the familiar affection and reassurance that she had come to depend on so much back home. It felt very good to have him here, although she realised that his presence threw up a new set of problems.

"How? When?" Esther said. "We've been in touch so often, and you never said."

"Wanted to surprise you!" Adam said, grinning from ear to ear.

"Does Lizzie know?" Esther asked.

"Nope! You know that she can't keep a secret to save her life!"

"True!" Esther said.

"I can't wait to tell her!" Esther said.

Unknown to Adam and Esther, Lizzie was facing her own drama. It would be many days before they would see their friend again.

It had started with an innocent visit to the souks. Lizzie and another nurse, Sandy, had gone to the souk where a very talented dressmaker would copy any garment and make a new one out of new material. Both of the girls had their abayas on but neither had their hair covered. Whether or not Western or non-Muslim women should cover their hair was a continual discussion, with the British Embassy advising that the covering of hair was a requirement of Muslims and as such non-Muslim British women did not need to wear a head covering.

The Matowa (the religious police) had other ideas, however, and would occasionally descend on the souks and challenge all those not wearing head coverings. On this day they started shouting at Lizzie and her friend. Both of them had head coverings in their bags and Sandy hastily put on hers. As the Matowas started to beat them on the legs shouting "cover your head!" in Arabic and English, Lizzie, with a temper that matched her flame red hair, snapped. She did the unthinkable. She pushed the Matowa and shouted at him, snatching the stick he had been beating her with, out of his hand.

The elderly man toppled over and hit the ground, hard. Within moments Lizzie found herself surrounded by police officers and thrown into the back of a police wagon.

It was later that evening that Esther heard what had happened. Sandy had come to her room, in a terrible state, white and shaking as she told Esther about Lizzie's arrest. The nurse had run for it while Esther was being arrested. She knew that she could do nothing to help and that it was more important that she got back to the hospital so that she could raise the alarm. She had let the hospital know and they in turn had informed the British embassy but the charges were serious. It was claimed that the elderly Matowa had been hurt as he fell.

Esther felt sick. After all she knew what the prisons were like and the thought of Lizzie languishing there was almost more than she could bear. Her first instinct was to go and tell Adam to get him to comfort her but they were in Saudi Arabia now and he lived in the hospital in a single flat and she would not be able to visit him there.

He could not come to her at Iskan, and if they met in a public place they would have to keep a distance between them. For the first time since she had arrived in this forbidding Kingdom, Esther felt very alone and afraid. She remembered a saying and hoped that she could somehow implant it in Lizzie's mind to give her strength and inform her of how much Esther loved her.

'Stop wasting your time on people who do not deserve your attention, trust me time spent with people who care about you is priceless.'

Meanwhile Lizzie was in hell. When she arrived at the prison female guards asked her to undress for 'inspection'... Lizzie was worried because she was wearing a sleeveless top and a short skirt under her abaya. She had no choice but to remove her abaya. The guards started to laugh pointing at her, obviously amused by her outfit.

Lizzie was ordered to strip to her underwear and the guards laughed harder still. It sounded very incongruous, their laughter in such a terrifying place and it did nothing for Lizzie's body issues as she heard them exchange what she assumed were derogatory comments in Arabic. Next, Lizzie was told to show her breasts in case there was anything hidden in her underwear.

The guards circled her looking her up and down muttering the word 'mashallaah' that Lizzie knew, bizarrely, was an Arabic term of appreciation. Finally, she was put into a cell in her own clothes. Few of the other women or the guards spoke English. At no point was Lizzie told what the process would be. She tried asking many times, begged to make a phone call, but she was ignored. The only thing that she could hope was that Sandy had got back to the hospital and raised alarm.

The prison was essentially a big hall with many rooms. In every room there were 6 bunk beds, other rooms had thin mattresses on the floor. There were about 40-50 prisoners in the area that Lizzie was put. Female prisoners offered Lizzie food and water. She soon realised that many like her, had been jailed for similar reasons. One woman had a newborn baby and quite a few small children were there in prison with their mothers.

In the big hall, there was a washroom with 5-6 toilets. Using the toilet, washing yourself, doing your dishes (people used cups to eat from) was all carried out in the same space. The smell was awful.

As night made way to morning, Lizzie was offered her first meal. A big tray was thrown on the floor and everyone had to grab their food with their hands from there.

Esther prayed hard that night. The next morning, she almost burst into tears with joy and gratitude as she saw the name of the maid of the Saudi dignitary on the list for clinic. The young Filipino woman was given a clean bill of health and Dr Hesham, who she had told about Lizzie spoke to the dignitary's wife to explain what had happened to Lizzie. She promised to tell her husband. Now all Esther could do was wait.

As the clinic door closed behind the Filipino maid and her mistress, Dr Hesham and Esther were alone together. Their eyes met and Esther felt herself flush.

"Thank you Hesham," she said softly.

He smiled at her and she could see in his eyes that he would like to have much more between them.

It was a few days later that Lizzie came back following her release from the filthy prison. Esther had made up her mind. She was going home.

Chapter Seven

Coming Home

If Esther thought that the time leading up to her leaving Saudi Arabia would go by quietly, she would have to think again! Out of prison, and back at work, Lizzie was spitting with indignation about her treatment and acting up as a result. She strode out through the souks as though she was daring another one of the Matowa to challenge her and she absolutely refused, ever, to cover her hair.

She was loud and obnoxious, at times drawing attention to herself and whomever she was with and that often included Esther. Esther was worried about her friend. Dr Hesham had offered to take them all out to a restaurant he knew where they could eat together undisturbed. The laws of the Kingdom were quite clear that men and women were not to be together if they were not related. But expats did go out to eat and Hesham had reassured them the restaurant would be safe.

Esther had been hard to convince.

"Are you quite sure Hesham?" She said, a worried frown on her face.

Hesham smiled.

"Hey don't spoil that beautiful face with a frown, would I really put you in danger?" They were alone in the clinic and he touched her cheek briefly. Esther blushed. Things had been a bit awkward between them since it had become clear how Hesham felt about her, and since Adam had arrived and she had told the young doctor that he had been her boyfriend back in the UK.

"Really?" He had said surprised, when she told him.

"You didn't mention anyone, and if you don't mind saying you don't really seem like a couple."

Esther thought about it. In fact, they did not feel like a couple. She had worried about that, about Adam's seeming lack of enthusiasm but he had never called off their relationship. It was a strange place to be. Were they or weren't they?

She and Adam could speak the most freely on the phone and they spent a lot of time talking over their experiences in the Kingdom but the young doctor still did not mention any plans or any future that included her.

Now the four of them made their way separately to the restaurant. Hesham and Adam in Hesham's car and Esther and Lizzie in a taxi. Esther could not help wondering what Hesham and Adam would talk about. She did not have to wonder about what Lizzie and she would talk about. Lizzie was on one of her rants, as usual.

"Look at them!" She bellowed as they passed a gaggle of Matowa standing beside one of the souks.

"Idiots! The lot of them! Nothing better to do than harass innocent people! *They* are the ones who should be banged up!"

Esther had learned that it was best to say nothing when Lizzie was off on one.

Esther hoped that by the time they reached the restaurant, her friend's mood would have improved, but that was not to be. The staff were very solicitous but the table that they were taken to was not to Lizzie's liking.

"Lizzie!" Esther said, "Hesham arranged this evening and he no doubt chose the table, *please* don't make a fuss."

Lizzie's raised voice was making head's turn. Luckily, Hesham and Adam arrived just in time.

They settled at the table, Lizzie with a face like thunder.

"Did you *really* choose this table?" She inquired of Hesham, a dangerous glint in her eye.

"Yes, don't you like it?" He said returning her gaze.

"Well I can't see anybody, all these bloody screens!"

"It is what they call intimate," Hesham said with a half-smile. "The better for us men to appreciate the beauty of our dining companions."

Despite herself, Lizzie could not help smiling and not for the first time Esther admired the way that Hesham had with people.

In the last weeks of her notice period at the hospital, Esther was transferred to the children's psychiatric ward. This was a grim place to work and she had to steel herself each day for her shift. One young girl in particular had captured her heart, a little girl called Huda. Huda was about 13 and had a horrible and deep groove over her skull from the top down to her neck. Esther had imagined the child had been the victim of a terrible accident but what she learned about her was far worse than any accident. According to custom, Huda had been married to a man much older than herself.

Because the girl had put up such a fight when her 50-year-old husband tried to sleep with her, it was assumed she was possessed and an ancient Bedouin cure was applied. A deep groove had been burned into the back of her head to let the demons out. When that only made things worse, she was admitted and then abandoned in the hospital by a family that had no further use for her. Esther knew about the practice of applying burns to the body as a method of distracting the patient from one pain by inflicting pain somewhere else. But the hell that this child must have endured took her breath away.

She would sit with Huda, who, because she had been in the hospital for so long, spoke some English. Esther would read her books, her favourite being the story of Heidi. How this little girl from the desert could relate to the life of a child living in such a different environment she knew hardly anything about was surprising and inspiring in equal measure. Nonetheless, Huda poured over the pictures of the little mountain cabin that Heidi lived in and the lush green mountain slopes with the goats and cattle roaming with bells around their necks.

Huda would smile up at Esther with pure joy in her eyes that would bring a lump to Esther's throat. For a little girl who had suffered so much, her young heart was still open to beauty and to love. When Esther asked what would become of Huda, no one seemed quite sure. She had been in the hospital now for over a year and could have been discharged, but there was nowhere for her to go.

Esther's thoughts immediately went to the family who had been so kind to Malaya, the Filipino prisoner who had been treated for breast cancer. She phoned Hesham. At first, he was reluctant to contact the couple who had been so kind, he was worried it would look like they were always asking them for favours, but Esther's instincts made her convince him that the couple would love the chance to help.

"I don't know Esther."

"Hesham, you know that they are kind-hearted people who are always willing to help."

"Yes they are but I don't want to take advantage of them."

"They wouldn't see it like that, I *know* they wouldn't."

"You are very passionate, Esther. Alright, I will get in touch with them." Hesham said.

Esther was sitting with Huda, reading Heidi two days later when in walked Hesham. With him were the Saudi couple and Malaya, who ran to Esther hugging her tightly. The couple smiled and approached Huda, who at the sight of a man in the thobe and gutra, the traditional Saudi robe and headdress, jumped off her bed and hid underneath it.

Immediately grasping what the problem was, the Saudi dignitary left the room. Coaxed out from under the bed, Huda smiled shyly at Malaya and at the Saudi lady whose kind face she immediately seemed to warm up to, even if slightly. Malaya sat on the bed next to Huda and put her arm around her. Soon, the Saudi lady had joined them and they were talking softly in Arabic. Esther had seen the look of shock on the woman's face when she saw the deep gash on Huda's head. Now that look had changed to one of compassion for this little girl who had suffered so much.

Hesham took Esther to one side and explained what the couple had in mind for Huda. She would come to the palace that they lived in and with Malaya and their own maids go back to school and learn how to work in the house and be a member of the household staff. She would be safe and looked after and she would be educated, trained and eventually able to earn her own money.

It was the answer to another prayer for Esther. She had worried that if nothing else was available for the young Bedouin girl, she might be put into an asylum and the more she knew Huda the more she was convinced that there was nothing wrong with her mentally, she just needed love and to be free of a life lived in fear.

That night before she went to sleep, Esther prayed her thanks to God. She felt his hand on everything that she did and again he had answered her prayers. She decided that she would tell Lizzie in the morning, go and surprise her before she got up for work. Lizzie was in one of the blocks in the main hospital, one of the huge blocks that overlooked the city. It was a single flat with its own cooking and washing facilities. Esther would have been moved too, if she was staying in the Kingdom.

The next morning, Esther arrived at the hospital campus to an eerie quietness. The working day was 7.30 to 4.00 and it was only six thirty. Esther had her own key to Lizzie's flat because she sometimes stayed there when Lizzie was away at one of the satellite hospitals so that she was nearer to work and got an extra half an hour in bed.

When she got to the door of the flat she thought she heard Lizzie's voice. Puzzled, she put her key in the door and opened it. She could still hear Lizzie talking and now a man answering her. It was not the way that Esther wanted to live her life but she knew that she and Lizzie were very different people and she tried not to judge her. She was about to leave, hoping that she had not been heard when a man emerged, stark naked, from Lizzie's bedroom. It took Esther a few moments to register who the man was. It was Adam.

Esther ran. She ran across the hospital campus all the way to the children's psychiatric ward. Her shift was not due to start for another hour but she knew that Huda would be awake. Today was the day that she was going to be discharged to her new home.

When she arrived, Huda was already dressed and sitting on her bed, looking through her Heidi book. She had been excited to know that she would be able to learn to read and write at her new home and although she would miss the staff that had looked after her so well on the ward, she seemed excited to start the new chapter in her young life.

As soon as the young Bedouin girl saw Esther's face,

she knew that something was wrong. She ran to Esther and threw her arms around her waist. Esther caught a glimpse of herself in the mirror. She was as white as the sheets on Huda's bed. Esther allowed Huda to lead her to the bed and they sat down.

The look of concern in the young girl's eyes was touching and Esther felt the tears begin to roll down her cheeks. Her mind was racing with the repercussions of what she now knew about her best friend and the man she had thought that one day she would marry. She tried to repeat a quote she had heard to herself, hoping it would calm her down.

Don't dwell in negativity and stress, take a step back and gather yourself and pray, fight through it and focus and have a positive mindset.

Huda wanted to know what was wrong.

"Nothing, Huda, I just had some bad news about a friend." She said, wiping her tears away. This was not the time for her own problems. It was a big day for Huda and she had to pull herself together for the girl. Esther had bought her a small bag for her belongings. Huda did not have much, just one dress and a few gifts that the staff had brought her and her books, including the Koran.

Esther tried to be upbeat in line with the young girl's excitement. She tried to keep her mind off what she had seen, what she knew, and once her shift started she threw herself into it. On his way to the Oncology ward, that was in the same building, Hesham popped in to see her and to say goodbye to Huda. Although she smiled brightly at him, Hesham rumbled Esther the minute he laid eyes on her.

"What's wrong Esther?"

Esther knew it was pointless to try and put him off and as he led her to the sluice room closing the door behind them, she told him what had happened.

Hesham gave a low whistle.

"Well, I didn't see that coming!" He said.

"Nor did I," Esther said trying to keep the bitterness

out of her voice.

"So, I don't understand, I thought you and Adam were, well, what they call an item?"

"It's a bit complicated, but yes, basically I thought that the fact that I was not like other girls, and refused to go to bed till I was married was OK with him, but obviously I was wrong."

"I'm sorry." Hesham said quietly and the floodgates opened. Esther began to sob and Hesham took her in his arms. Despite the fact that they would be in very grave trouble if they were caught, the young doctor could not watch this young nurse whom he had come to care for so much, breaking her heart. He held Esther and rocked her back and forward slightly until her sobs subsided. Then he wiped the tears off her cheeks and smiled at her.

"Whatever has happened, it has shown you the true nature of the people around you, and for that you should be grateful."

"I can't believe that my best friend, Lizzie would do this to me." Esther said sadly.

Hesham smiled at her.

"I remember how your friend was when we went out to dinner. She is one of those people who act on their impulse, often without thinking at all of what the result of their actions will be. Don't be too hard on her. I am quite sure that her love for you as a friend is genuine."

"Going to bed with someone repeatedly is not something you do on impulse and I am quite sure that was not the first time," Esther said.

"Maybe not but maybe there is something deeper between them. I have to say that I was never really convinced by you and Adam as a couple." Adam said and Esther looked at him sharply.

"You did not seem to have a deep connection, even allowing for the fact that you were in Saudi Arabia and had to keep your distance. And I don't believe that a relationship has to be physical to succeed. Feelings can be intense and genuine even without sex." Esther was silent. Hesham was only echoing the thoughts she had had about herself and Adam, the feeling she had that their relationship was not the way that a committed relationship should be.

A picture she had seen came to her mind. It was by Verkennen and showed a woman clinging to the skeleton of a man. The caption, that she had never forgotten read: *A profound sketch of a woman giving her all to a man that can offer her nothing. The transfer of energy is real. If you are continually surrounded by, interacting with, having sex with, pouring your feelings and yourself into an empty person eventually they will suck you dry. Know your worth and surround yourself with people, places and things that won't leave you spiritually empty, on skin and bone.*

An hour later they saw Huda off and Esther threw herself into the rest of her shift. At four when she left the ward, Lizzie was waiting for her. The girl looked terrible, she had obviously been crying and her eyes were puffy. Esther wanted to just walk past her but despite herself, her heart went out to her friend.

"My flat?" Lizzie said and Esther nodded.

They walked in silence back to the flat. Inside Lizzie started to talk immediately.

"I am so sorry Esther, we were going to tell you, I swear we were."

"How long?" Esther said.

"Since Adam came out here."

Esther closed her eyes. She thought about the many times she had been with her friend and Adam together or alone and had no idea. It hurt.

"The thing is, Esther, I think this is the real thing. It's not just a fling. I mean it; I think Adam is 'the one.'"

There was silence for a moment. Then Lizzie said. "I have to go to Al Kharj Hospital for a month and Adam is going there too. I'll be back before you go. Can you think about it and then we can talk when I get back?"

Esther looked at her friend. She was not the mess that Esther would have expected her to be. She really seemed to be collected, and when she spoke about herself and Adam she seemed to have a quiet maturity that Esther had not seen before.

Esther nodded and quietly let herself out of Lizzies flat. As she walked away, she thought of a saying that had often sustained her.

Life is like a book, some chapters are sad; some are happy and some exciting. But if you never turn the page you will never know what the next chapter holds.

Well, Esther thought to herself, she was ready to turn the page.

Chapter Eight

Home again, new start, new love

Being back home after more than two years away took more getting used to than Esther thought it would. She had not been home during her stay in Riyadh because she wanted to save every penny she could. Her position came with a travel allowance, that if not used, was paid in cash and although she missed her mum and Levi dreadfully, she wanted the money for her future and for her mother. Esther could not wait to find a course to train as a lawyer but she thought about an inspirational thought she had read.

Appreciate where you are in your journey, even if it is not where you want to be, every season serves a purpose.

Levi and her mother were at the airport to meet her.

"Esther, Esther!" Levi shouted through the bustle of arriving passengers. At first Esther did not recognise her brother.

"Levi? Is that you?" Esther ran into his arms. He had grown about eighteen inches since she left and he towered over her. Esther laughed as her mother joined the embrace and then they all cried together with the joy of being reunited.

Esther noticed instantly that her mother looked more relaxed and had even put on a little weight, and she felt so pleased that she had been able to ease her mother's workload by sending her money from Saudi.

Esther was determined not to waste any time before she got back to work. Her old hospital welcomed her back with open arms and within weeks she felt as though she had never been away. But there was something different. She spent every waking hour when she was not at work researching courses where she could qualify as a lawyer.

Esther had heard nothing from Adam or Lizzie since she had come home and it was the only cloud on her horizon. She had heard from Hesham but they both knew that there was no future for them and their contact gradually faded away. Now that time had passed she felt fine about the fact that her best friend and Adam had got together. After all, hadn't she always had her own doubts about her and Adam? There was no denying that she had. Now without the constant wondering about their relationship, she was free to concentrate on her future, and the thought of it was very exciting.

Levi was doing well too. He seemed keen to spend a lot of his free time with his sister.

"How is school going?" Esther asked him.

"Not bad, I decided I want to go to college and study to be a plumber or be a pro footballer"

Esther's eyebrows shot up.

"Hey that's great Levi, plumbers are always in demand."

"Yea. That's what I thought."

"What about the footie?"

Levi lit up.

"We won the last three matches with all the goals scored by," he punched the air, "moi!"

"Well, I'll just have to come and see for myself at your next match!" Esther laughed.

"There is a chance that I might be getting a try out for Arsenal." He said quietly, as though if he said it out loud he might jinx it.

"What? Levi that is amazing. Tell me all about it!"

For Ruth it was wonderful having Esther back. She was so proud of her daughter and the contributions she had sent from Saudi had made a huge difference to her life. One thing she noticed however was that something had obviously happened between Esther and Lizzie. She had asked about Lizzie earlier.

"How is Lizzie? She's not thinking of coming home?" She asked Esther.

Esther shrugged. "I don't think so for the time being, at least."

"And Adam, how is he enjoying life as a doctor in Riyadh?"

"Fine, I think."

"Hmm, you don't seem to know an awful lot about Lizzie and Adam considering you were all out there together." Ruth said.

"Well mum, you know how it is, we were all busy doing different jobs in different parts of the hospital."

Ruth looked at her daughter. Clearly there was something wrong, but for now she would hold her tongue. Esther would tell her if she wanted to, or upon her insistence.

Esther could not hide her delight for being in church. It was great to be amongst familiar faces and there were some new ones too. One in particular seemed very interested in getting to know Esther. His name was John Sanderson and Esther thought he was about as perfect as a man could be. He was kind and caring with a lovely calming presence, he was a really committed family man and was also very successful in banking.

As they walked back from church, John took Esther's hand and began to talk about his business.

"I have so many plans for my future, Esther, I know I can go to the top, and all I need to make that dream come true is a good woman by my side."

Esther laughed at his old-fashioned way of speaking but her heart fluttered. There was definitely something about this self-assured and kind man that made her heart beat faster.

One thing that Esther did notice about John was that his knowledge of Christianity did not seem to be as deep as his outward appearance indicated. Whereas Esther knew her Bible inside out, John seemed to have very big gaps in his knowledge. In church, his deep and melodic voice would dominate other voices as he sang his praises to the Lord and Esther saw the admiring glances that he got. He was a handsome and a charming man, but not one that was very knowledgeable in his religion.

Far from this being a turn-off to Esther, she thought that it would be a wonderful way for them to spend time together, to know each other better. She would be the one to teach him in areas where his knowledge was sketchy. She was very happy to think that she could do that, and confident that sharing the experience would bring them closer together.

It worked, she and John spent many hours together pouring over the scriptures and enjoying the Bible's teachings. John was an eager student and Esther felt her heart swell, delighted that she could be the one to let him share the joy that her knowledge of the Bible and of the Lord had given her.

Ruth and Levi loved John. He was always smiling and willing to have a kick about with Levi. It was he who took Levi for his try out at Arsenal football ground and he was there with them when Levi heard that he was being offered a place on the Arsenal Youth Team. The family and John danced around the lounge celebrating and Levi was in seventh heaven. The weeks turned into months and Esther relaxed into her friendship with John.

They both worked hard, but any time they had, they spent together. Esther thought that she was not ready to think about another relationship after what had happened with Adam but bit by bit, she realised that she was falling in love with her tall and handsome friend. So on the day that he took her face in his hands and kissed her gently on the lips she felt herself respond, with every part of her heart and soul.

"Oh Esther, you are so wonderful, so gentle, so…." John shook his head and she saw tears in his eyes. "I'm in love with you." He whispered.

Esther looked up at him and said,

"I love you too John."

They clung together and as his warm mouth explored hers, she felt herself melt. She had always said that she would be pure when she got married, but with John she knew it was going to be very difficult to keep her resolve.

Ruth noticed the change in Esther and understood that her daughter was in love. Esther was a girl who played things quite close to her chest so Ruth was content to say nothing and just enjoy the sight of her daughter happy, singing and almost skipping in her joy. Ruth liked John and she began to hope that maybe she would be able to welcome him into the family as an official son in law.

It was on a late summer afternoon that Esther got a phone call from Lizzie. Her friend's voice shook with emotion as she said,

"Esther?"

"Lizzie." Esther could barely talk; she felt such mixed emotions at the sound of her friend's voice.

"How are you Esther?"

"I'm fine, how about you…. and Adam?"

There was a pause.

"We're fine. Actually that was why I called you. We got married Esther, me and Adam got married."

There was another silence then Esther said.

"Hey! Get you two! When did you do that? *Where* did you do that?"

Lizzie gave a ragged sigh of relief and started to half laugh and half cry.

"In Cyprus, two months ago. Oh Esther, bless you, dear sweet Esther, I was so afraid you would hate me, hate us."

"Don't be silly, I'm pleased for you! Congratulations! Is Adam there?"

"Hi Esther." Adams voice sounded emotional too.

"Congratulations, I am very pleased for you. Really I am."

"You really are one in a million Esther. We are coming home in a month, we'd love to see you."

"Of course!" Esther found she really did look forward to seeing her friends.

"OK, we'll keep in touch Esther."

"Definitely! Bye Adam, bye Lizzie!"

"Bye Esther, love you loads!" And they were gone.

Esther had told John about what had happened with Lizzie and Adam and he had been sympathetic, if not a little wary, in case Esther might not be over Adam. But she had reassured him. Now, when she told him that her friends were married and coming home, Esther was surprised that he was not more excited. When she told him John simply shrugged.

"Well I suppose you are quite busy, at work at the hospice at home and with me, you won't have much time to spend with them. The trouble with you Esther is that you are too trusting, too forgiving. I would certainly not entertain anyone who had done to me what those two have done to you."

Esther was surprised.

"Our Lord teaches us that we must forgive. And as well as that, I told you that there was nothing really serious between me and Adam."

John shrugged again.

"Yes but there are some things that are more difficult to forgive and I think that for a best friend, Lizzie behaved very poorly. You might forgive her, and it is right that you do, but why surround yourself with negative people, backstabbers who are not real friends. I'm only thinking of you, Esther."

Esther said nothing. It was clear that John was not keen on seeing neither Adam nor Lizzie and she felt a stinging disappointment as her hopes of showing John off to her friends evaporated. She knew that John was only thinking of her but it was sad that it didn't look like the people she cared for the most in the world would be friends. John seemed happiest when they were with his family, or hers. Esther reassured herself that she was lucky to have such a family orientated man.

At the beginning of autumn John booked a short holiday for them. Esther knew that it would mean sharing a room but John reassured her that they would not go any further than she wanted. He respected the fact that she was a virgin.

John had booked them into a B and B in Plymouth in Devon and Esther delighted in the fact that from their room they could see the sea, shining in bright autumn sunshine. On the large area that spread across the seafront called "The Hoe" they walked, talked and laughed. The tourists had gone for the season now and it seemed to them as though they had the place to themselves.

They crossed the river Tamar to Cornwall on a small foot ferry and walked under the tress Mount Edgcumbe Country Park kicking up the fallen leaves and chasing each other with handfuls of gold, orange and crimson to throw like confetti. Suddenly, John grabbed her hand. Standing her in front of him he went down on one knee. He reached into his pocket and pulled out a small box. Esther felt as though her heart had stopped.

Opening the box John looked up at her, with love in his eyes.

"Esther, will you do me the honour of becoming my wife?"

Esther stared at the exquisite ring open-mouthed. It was beautiful and she felt tears spring to her eyes.

"Yes," she whispered, "yes!"

John leapt up and gathered her up in his arms, swinging her around in the swirling autumn leaves. They laughed and kissed and they cried with joy. Esther phoned her mother and told her. Ruth was delighted and even Levi who could normally only think or talk about his place in the Arsenal Youth Team seemed genuinely delighted that he would have a brother at last.

"Hey cool!" He said. "Congrats you two!"

Later that night, Esther lay, facing John on their double bed. He kissed the ring on her finger and then touched her face and kissed her lips. The warmth from his body and the passion in his kiss made her head swim and the now familiar feelings of desire overtook her. As his hands gently caressed her she made a decision. This was going to be 'the night'.

This was the man that she was going to marry. She could give herself to John, she wanted to give herself, her breathing was coming fast now and her body was responding to him. As she looked into his eyes she saw the question there. She knew that he would not mind if she said no, but she was not going to. Almost imperceptibly, Esther nodded and John smiled at her with tears in his eyes.

John was gentle and kind and for the first time in her life Esther knew what it was to give herself to a man. Her love for John was overwhelming and when it was over and they lay in each other's arms, he kissed her on the head.

She said a prayer of thanks to God for bringing him into her life. She remembered something she had read.

A kiss on the head after sex is just for you. He gets nothing out of it, he knows it is not going to turn you on, and it gives him no real pleasure. That is a kiss that comes from nothing but sweetness and care.

The news of their wedding was received with great celebration at the church. The plans were being made and people were genuinely excited that two of the most loved of the congregation were going to be married. Ruth was beside herself. In John she saw a man that would make her daughter happy, someone who could be a strong male role model in the family. Levi already hero-worshipped John and Ruth could see the great affect that he had on her son.

In the middle of the preparations, Lizzie and Adam came back. Now that she and John were engaged, Esther was keen for them all to meet. But she remembered John's reaction when she had told them about her friend's visit. Now she broached the subject tentatively.

"Lizzie and Adam are back on holiday, I thought it would be nice for us all to go out for a meal?"

"Yes, of course, why not?" John said and Esther felt relief wash over her. In her mind she repeated the words that had become important to her:

You deserve someone who never stops trying to show how much you mean to them, even after they have you.

Esther was so touched that he was doing this, just for her, when she knew he really didn't want to.

Two nights later they met at the local Nandos, Lizzie and Esther hugged each other, tears running down their faces. They had missed each other. Clearly, theirs was a friendship that would never be broken.

As they sat down, the waitress came to ask if they would like drinks. Lizzie and Adam exchanged glances and then Lizzie said,

"Not for me thanks, you can't drink when you are expecting!"

"Lizzie!" Esther was out of her seat and beside her friend in a second, hugging her. "This is fantastic news.

When is the baby due?"

"Actually it is still very early days, a honeymoon baby. The baby is due next year in the spring."

"Congratulations!" Esther said and John added his best wishes.

Esther thought that John was being quite reserved but she put it down to the fact that he did not know Lizzie and Adam and that her and her two old friends were probably a bit full on.

Once Lizzie and Adam had gone back, it was full steam ahead for Esther and John's Christmas wedding. Esther was quite surprised by the fact that John's mother and sisters seemed to take over the arrangements, reassuring Ruth and Esther that they wanted to make sure that the whole thing did not stress them out too much.

Esther did not even have a choice of the flowers, before she knew it, they were all chosen. Even at her appointment to choose her wedding dress, John's sisters and his mother's voices all but drowned out Ruth and Esther's. Esther tried to raise her concerns with John.

"Your mum, Cheryl and Lynn seem very certain about what they want to see at the wedding. I kind of feel like my voice is getting lost."

"Don't be silly, baby, they are only trying to help you, my goodness with work and everything you certainly could not manage it all, besides which they all have excellent taste, I trust what they say completely."

"And you don't trust me?" Esther said quietly.

John took her in his arms,

"Of course I do baby! But they are trying to help and if you trust them like I do, you are going to be thrilled, really, I know you will!"

And Esther could see there was no point in arguing. The important thing was that she was marrying the man of her dreams. She was going to be Mrs Sanderson.

Chapter Nine
Married Life, Married Strife

The wedding was wonderful. The early December day was bright and crisp and Esther looked beautiful in her wedding gown. As Esther looked around the well-loved faces that filled the church to celebrate her marriage to John, she felt tears well up in her eyes. She felt breathless with happiness as she walked down the aisle on Levi's arm. As she passed her mother, they smiled, a smile that only a mother and daughter would understand. Theirs had been a difficult road but they had made it and now life was being good to both of them.

The service passed in a whirl of happiness and emotion and as they emerged from the church, a few flakes of snow were falling that Esther knew would make the photos look great. Suddenly a familiar voice caught her ear.

"Esther! Over here Esther!"

It was Lizzie. She ran and threw her arms around her friend.

"Hey, you look soooo good!" Lizzie said.

"Lizzie, this is such a surprise," Esther hugged her back. "Let me get the photos done and we can catch up!"

As they posed for the photos, John whispered to her.

"You look so beautiful; I am so proud that you are my wife. I love you."

"I love you too." Esther thought her heart might burst with happiness.

She tried to catch up with Lizzie as she had promised, but it seemed that John's family had other ideas and monopolised her time with their extended family from the UK and back home in Ghana. Before she knew it, it was time to leave for the honeymoon and the most she could do was to wave to her own mother, Levi and Lizzie as John and his mother bundled her into the taxi that would take them to the airport.

The honeymoon was a Caribbean cruise, and Esther loved it. The chance to wake up to a different exotic island every day without packing and unpacking was great and she felt that it was the most romantic and perfect time that she and John could have had. And as John and she stood together watching the sun go down he said to her,

*"If she is amazing she won't be easy, and if she is easy she won't be amazing. If she's worth it, you won't give up, and if you give up **you** are not worthy. The truth is that everyone has the potential to hurt you. You have just got to find the ones worth suffering for."*

John looked at her with tears in his eyes. "That is how I feel about you my darling wife."

Esther thought she could not be happier.

They had been looking for a flat before they got married but without any luck. As they boarded the flight back to the UK, Esther said,

"What are we going to do about somewhere to live?"

"Well, the wedding rather took over in the last months but after we get back we'll make a big effort. In the meantime there are no worries, we'll live at home in my room. Mum and Dad are happy to have us."

Esther was speechless. There was no discussion, it was just what had been decided but without any consultation with her.

"Oh I kind of thought we might stay at mum's, there is a lot more room there, and the bedroom that she used to let out to lodgers has its own bathroom, it's almost like a bedsit."

John waved her suggestion away.

"Don't worry baby, it's all arranged. It will be a bit of a crush but we are all family now, aren't we? Besides, dad and mum thought that this would be the best idea, and they are always right. It's a lot closer to my work as well."

"But not mine," Esther said.

"Yes, I did think of that but as my sisters pointed out, because you work shifts, you never have to contend with the rush hour."

"Cheryl and Lynn said that?"

"Yes, isn't it great that they are so thoughtful?"

As the cabin lights dimmed for the overnight flight, Esther tried to ignore the little worm of anger that was burrowing into her brain. She had to concentrate on finding a course for the next year now, and after all, what did it matter where they lived? It wouldn't be for long anyway. As she drifted off to sleep a saying came to her mind.

Life is the most difficult exam, many people fail because they try to copy others, not realising that everyone has a different question paper.

Her life was about to change and she had new responsibilities and dreams, it was time to take her place in the world, she was going places!

Life with the in laws was a test. Esther soon realised that John seemed totally unable to make a decision without consulting his mother, father and even his younger sisters. When she was on early shifts, she stayed at home with her mother, and Esther found herself looking forward to those shifts.

At John's parent's home, she was 'managed' all the time. As she looked for university courses, the sisters made suggestions and decided what would be best for her. Her mother in law stood over her when she ironed John's shirts (something that she had been told it was her duty to do) and made suggestions. John's father flatly rejected anything Esther suggested for she and John to look at. Even the dog seemed to delight in ripping up any item of clothing she left lying around.

Esther prayed and looked on line for answers. She found what she needed in the words of Eric Stanley:

Gonna buy a house? Close your mouth.
Going to buy a car? Close your mouth.
Are you getting married? Close your mouth.
Going on a trip? Close your mouth.
Going to do courses or college? Close your mouth.
Was promoted at work?? Close your mouth.
99 % of the time the reason that our dreams/visions don't come true when they are supposed to is because we open our mouth too soon to the wrong people at the wrong time, we were wrong to share our projects with people who claim to be "friends". The envy and the low key jealousy is enough for people to feed off of and tear down what COULD HAVE BEEN before it evens happens so... Close your mouth and let "God" work everything out at the right time and on time!

The majority of your "friends", want to see you well, But never better than them. Just to warn you! Even family members can have a hidden envy but they can't stop what God has for you!

Esther kept her head down and looked for courses. She had decided that what she wanted to study was human rights combined with criminology - a double degree that included corporate and financial law. She would still have to do some nursing shifts because it would be tight. She had just sent the first round of applications off when John dropped his bombshell.

They were eating dinner, and John's father and mother were cooing over him as usual, telling him how wonderful he was, how he was wasted in banking, when he said it.

"Actually you are right mummy, daddy, and I appreciate your faith in me. I've decided I am going to do a master's degree in finance!"

As Esther dropped her knife and fork on her plate with a clatter, the rest of John's family rose from the table to give him a round of applause.

"Aren't you pleased for me?" John asked her

"Yes of course, but with me in education too, what are we going to do for money?" Esther tried to smile.

"Esther!" Her mother in law spoke sharply. "Whatever you think you are doing, John has to be the priority. He is the breadwinner, the man of the family; I am really surprised that your mother has not given you a better idea of how important the African man of the house is."

Esther bit her tongue. The man of the house! That was a joke. They did not even have their own place, and not likely to either, with neither of them earning a proper salary. Had this been his plan all along? To live with his folks - never to branch out with her to their own place?

But her mother in law was not finished.

"I wonder how important it really is that you go to university Esther? You have a perfectly good nursing job, a good job for a wife and maybe in the future, a mother. The benefits, the maternity leave, and all those things you have to think about. And it's not as though you are doing further qualifications in nursing. Frankly, I think this law business is really a rather silly idea. And daddy agrees, don't you daddy?"

John's father nodded and his sisters said,
"We agree."

Esther looked at John for support, but he was looking down at his hands. Getting up from the table Esther ran upstairs to her room. She needed to calm down.

Breathing deeply, she sat on the edge of the bed. She felt trapped and a deep sense of foreboding was taking hold of her. This was not what it was supposed to be like. She and John were supposed to be a united front, working together to make a future for themselves. She had shared her dreams with John and he knew how much her study plans meant to her. It was the reason she had stayed in Saudi to earn enough money to fund university.

Esther prayed. And three days later it seemed as though God had heard her. A cousin of John's was offering them a brand new flat to live in at a very small rent if they would keep an eye on the five other flats that he owned in the modern block he had developed

At last they had their own place and could really start their life as husband and wife. Esther took time off work to decorate and make the flat a home for them. But if she had thought that John would be as excited as she was, she was mistaken. He barely seemed to notice the curtains she had picked out, the rugs she had chosen and the pictures she had put up on the wall.

All he could think about was the course that he was going to do. And if she thought that moving out of his family home would mean she would see a lot less of his family, she was mistaken again. She would come back from a shift, exhausted and wanting to put her feet up, and nine times out of ten one or both of John's sister's would be there, usually with his mother and father.

They would expect Esther, as an African wife, to cook them a meal and entertain them. Esther had just started her legal training at university and needed every minute she could to study. Because John could not work at his banking job, and study at the same time, she was now responsible for financing their life. So as well as her study Esther had to take agency shifts that took her all around London. One thing that she soon found out was that as an agency nurse you were the lowest of the low, you got all the grotty jobs to do. Esther found herself dipping into the money that she had so carefully put aside from her earnings in Saudi.

Ruth noticed the change in her daughter. Esther constantly looked tired and was short-tempered. She seemed to be retreating into herself. Even Levi had noticed.

"Hey mum, what's with Esther? I phoned her to ask her to come and see me play this weekend and she bit my head off. At least John is coming."

"Well, Levi, it's tough for them both studying and not much money coming in."

"Well, if John can find the time, why can't she?"

Ruth did not answer. She knew that John was not working as well as studying like Esther but she tried not to judge. The young couple must run their lives as they saw fit. But there was no doubt that Esther looked ready to drop.

As the months passed, Esther realised that John was not doing well on his course. He was failing modules and constantly being called in to see his tutors. Esther did what she could to help him checking his work for spelling mistakes and doing her best to understand and help him with his work.

She was determined not to draw on her savings any more than she had to and she took on as many nursing shifts as she could, working night shifts and going to university during the day. Esther kept going by imagining how much better things were going to be when John had graduated, if he ever graduated. Her husband was lazy. There was no doubt about that. They barely spoke and when they did it was acrimonious.

One day as she was getting dressed to go to university and John was still in bed, Esther said,

"John, would you do some shopping this afternoon?

We need just about everything and I will have to go straight from university to work."

John sat up, shook his head and tutted.

"You know what Esther, a good wife would have this kind of thing under control, you have responsibilities to the home and to your husband."

Esther took a deep breath. She tried hard to think of a saying that she took strength from:

Have more than you show, speak less than you know.

Her attempts to calm herself were not working.

"Yes, I would normally but it is difficult with study and work." She said through clenched teeth.

"Oh my goodness Esther, I am so tired of you whining about what you have to do. You live almost rent-free in a home provided by one of my family members, my sisters and my mother and father do all they can to help us...."

Esther could not hold her tongue any longer.

"Help?" She shouted. "They sit on that settee and judge me, that's what they do, they don't help! You always take their side and you never show me any respect. I am so tired, so tired of it all!" Esther collapsed in tears on the bed.

For a moment John was silent and then Esther felt his hands pulling her towards him.

"Now then Esther, I know you don't mean that, you are overtired. There's no need to get upset baby, of course I will do the shopping." John knew that he had to be careful here, he could not afford for Esther to collapse, she was the only one keeping them afloat.

Esther was so desperate for affection and to feel appreciated that even this hollow victory seemed like a massive positive to her.

Two days later she returned to find the tiny flat full of people. She had just finished a 12-hour shift and she wanted to sleep.

"There you are baby!" John said giving her a hug. "It's Cheryl's birthday so I've invited a few people around. I knew you would be back soon and I have promised them some of your delicious blueberry pancakes. I bought the ingredients for you," He finished proudly.

Esther was speechless. She looked at the eggs and flour and blueberries that had been dumped in the tiny kitchenette and closed her eyes for a moment. When she opened them, everyone was looking at her expectantly. Quietly she crossed the room, went into her bedroom and shut the door quietly behind her. She leaned on it listening to the voices of John's family.

"Your wife does not even say hello?"

"Is she coming out to cook for us?"

"Oh my poor brother, what you have to put up with, it's shameful."

Suddenly the door was shoved open and Esther fell forward onto the bed.

"Esther what the hell are you doing? How could you embarrass me like this? Go out and apologise and cook the pancakes. You are my wife, you have duties, people expect you to show them respect in my house, and offer them hospitality."

"John," Esther said softly, pulling herself fully onto the bed with her last ounce of strength. "I have not slept in 24 hours. I am too tired to speak let alone cook pancakes. I'm sorry." And with that he eyes closed and she was instantly fast asleep.

When she woke up the flat was dark and empty. For some time, Esther lay in the dark with tears rolling down her cheeks. She knew that she had committed a terrible sin in the eyes of her husband, shamed him in his home. A saying that she had held on to since she met John came into her mind.

You may have been overlooked, but who God has for you will understand that you are a blessing and not a burden.

At this moment in time, Esther very much doubted that John saw her as a blessing.

She was aware that his family had a low opinion of her. They thought she was a complainer, and disrespectful to their king of a son. They thought he was a wonderful man, everyone did. But the difference was that John was living life on his terms, doing the bare minimum he needed, to get by, while Esther did the rest.

Again, Esther's prayers were answered when she was at her lowest ebb. John came home and apologised for putting too much on her. He realised it was too much of a strain for her and he had told his family to call before they came round.

And life went on. It was exhausting and her money was dwindling fast but she and John argued less. It was a blessing of sorts.

Chapter Ten
Almost an end and a ne beginning

As the months became years, Esther felt as though her life was reduced to work, study and sleep. John had kept his word and his family now usually called before they came. When they did see Esther, they made no secret of their contempt for a wife who did not keep her home pristine, and who insisted on working and studying when she should be caring for her husband and her home.

One afternoon when Esther was not working and not at London City university, and was grabbing some valuable study time at home, her mother in law arrived at the door. Instead of inviting the older woman in, Esther held on to the door and said,

"John is not in at the moment, if you come back this evening, he will be."

"Now then, Esther, what is this? Not inviting your mother in law into your husband's home? I know that I did not *call in advance,*" the older woman's voice dripped sarcasm "but in fact it was you that I wanted to speak to."

"I am very busy at the moment." Esther said.

Her mother in law rudely pushed past Esther into the little flat.

"Not busy tidying up and keeping house like a good wife should though?" She said as she looked around the flat, her tone showing how much she despised her daughter in law.

"Do you know what, Abena?" Esther used her mother in law's first name knowing that the older woman hated it. She expected Esther to call her mummy, just as John did. But to Esther the term 'mummy' was one that did not belong to someone who saw her as a constant disappointment and probably should not be used by anyone who was over the age of 10, either.

Ignoring her mother in law's disapproving look, Esther said again, "You know what Abena, your precious son makes far more mess than I do, God knows I am never here, when I am not working I am at the university, while he loafs around here and makes all this mess."

Abena stared at her daughter in law, open-mouthed. But Esther was not finished.

"None of you seem to realise what I have to do and how little time I have for anything. If your son makes the mess, why shouldn't he clear it up?"

Abena smiled a cruel cold smile.

"Esther, you are a wife, that is your first priority. If you did not think you could manage everything then you should not have married my son and you certainly should not have taken on this silly university course."

Esther closed her eyes. It was pointless arguing with her mother in law. The only thing that she was interested in was John and making sure that her little prince was kept on the pedestal that she and his father had put him on.

Esther repeated a quote to herself that she had memorised and that helped her in times like this.

May you have enough happiness to make you sweet, enough trials to make you strong, enough sorrow to keep you human and enough hope to make you happy. The happiest of people don't necessarily have the best of everything; they just make the most of everything that comes along their way. The brightest future will always be based on a forgotten past; you can't go forward in life until you let go of your past failures and heartaches.

"What are you muttering?" Abena asked angrily. Esther opened her eyes and looked into Abena's vicious glare.

"Do you know what my girl?" Abena said with venom in her voice. "I am beginning to think that the problem here is that you are not quite right in the head. To speak to your elders and betters as you do, to disrespect your husband's family and neglect John and his needs, maybe the problem is the fact you are damaged goods. Your own father did not stick around so you have no idea how to behave properly. Your mother is decent enough but obviously something has gone wrong."

Esther felt fury overtake her. Without saying another word, she propelled her mother in law to the door, opened it and shoved her outside.

Standing with her back on the door, Esther heard her mother shouting insults at her from outside. She breathed deeply for a few moments and then locked the door and went back to her books.

The repercussions were almost immediate. John returned home and he was angrier than Esther had ever seen him. They rowed and though not for the first time in their marriage, Esther felt afraid that this really could be the end. She knew that she was right and she could not understand how this man who had once professed to love her more than his life could be so callous as to always take the side of his family against her.

John hated the fact that his family found so much to criticise in his wife. It was important to him that he should be seen, to his parents, to be perfect in every way and having a wife who fell so short of the mark was an irritation and a disappointment to him. Now, as he looked at Esther, tears running down her face, John felt some of the old feeling he had, resurface. He crossed to her and put his arms around her.

"Come on baby, let's not fight over this. I know that you are busy and I will try to help out more. We're almost there, I am going to graduate soon and you just after that, and then it will be plain sailing. You'll have your job as a lawyer saving the planet, and I'll be teaching at the university."

Despite herself, Esther smiled. She hated how desperate she was for even the smallest validation from John. Now she clung to him as he kissed her on the lips. Before she knew it, he had scooped her up and taken her to the bedroom. They made love tenderly, tears still streamed from Esther's eyes and John kissed them away. Esther felt the love that she had for John re-surface and bloom like a summer rose in her soul. As they lay in each other's arms, she listened to him talking softly about the future and she believed him. She needed to believe him.

Two months later the result of that tender afternoon of lovemaking showed up in a pregnancy test. Esther was expecting a baby. She and John had made love so infrequently before that afternoon that she had stopped taking the pill, relieved, as it had made her feel unwell.

Instead, they had kept condoms but with such infrequent need for them, neither of them could remember where. Besides which neither of them had wanted to ruin the highly charged moment, by looking for a condom.

Lizzie was the first person that Esther told. She was back from Saudi with her beautiful little girl Tessa to ask Esther if she would be the child's Godmother. Esther was delighted. She had only seen Lizzie, Adam and Tessa a handful of times since the child's birth and she missed having her friend to confide in whenever she needed to unload. Lizzie was staying with Ruth and Levi and Esther spent as much time around there as she could. Levi was a man now and working hard at his football career.

Ruth joked that he would soon be able to keep them all in the manner to which they would like to become accustomed, with his mega football wages. It had started as a joke but as every month passed, the man that Levi had become was inching closer to his goal of a place in the first team.

Esther was so proud of him but sad that her own problems and punishing schedule had kept her from spending more time with her mother and brother. John did spend a lot of time with Levi and for Esther that was a huge blessing. Levi idolised him and was so proud to take him to the matches he played.

Lizzie and Esther were sitting together in the park while Levi pushed a delighted Tessa on the swings.

"So come on then Esther, spill!" Lizzie said.

"I don't know what you mean?" Esther said.

"Oh come on girlie, I've known you long enough now, something is up."

"Nope, still not with you." Esther said.

"Ok let me guess then. I know, you've won the lottery!"

Esther laughed, "I wish!"

"Oh OK, maybe then – you're pregnant!" Lizzie said triumphantly.

Esther was shocked.

"How did you know?"

"Ah never question the powers of mystic Lizzie!" Her friend said. "So are you?"

Esther nodded.

"And you were going to tell me - when?"

"Well mystic Lizzie, I didn't really get the chance, you were so quick with your diagnosis!"

Lizzie hugged her friend. "I am so delighted for you Esther. I bet John is beside himself."

"I haven't told him yet. I only found out myself for sure, yesterday." Esther said quietly.

"OMG!" Lizzie shouted.

The truth was that John was an unknown quantity as far as telling him that he was going to be a father. Esther really did not have any idea how he was going to react. She found out that evening as they sat down to a meal together. It was her favourite and the only dish that John ever cooked for her, a goat curry. Now as she looked at the steaming food on the plate in front of her, she felt herself urge. Dashing for the toilet, she just made it.

John stood behind her in the bathroom door.

"Hey baby, what's up? Are you sick?" His voice was concerned.

He took her arm and led her back to the table. Esther pushed the food away and looked at him.

"I am sure the food is wonderful, John." She said, her voice shaking. "It's not that, it's…." Esther took a deep breath, "I'm pregnant."

For a moment there was silence as John's eyes widened. Then a smile started at the corner of his lips and spread to his whole face and he was on his feet scooping Esther up and twirling her around.

"Really? We're having a baby?"

"Yes! John please put me down, I really do feel queasy!"

"Oh of course. I'm sorry baby, are you all right? Come on, sit here, are you warm enough, shall I get you a blanket? What can I do?"

Esther laughed. She was so relieved that John was so happy.

"At last I can make my parents happy and give them a grandchild!" He said and instantly Esther felt her happiness evaporate. Was that what he wanted their child for - to satisfy his parents' desire for a grandchild? He had picked up his phone now and she was forgotten as he rang his parents and anyone else he could think of at that moment. Before he had finished the last call, his parents, who had been the first call, were at the door.

John's parents and his sisters clamoured to hug and kiss and congratulate him, his mother and sisters crying with joy. No one took any notice at all of Esther and making an excuse, that nobody heard, she retired to the bedroom.

John and his family celebrated long into the night and his phone did not stop ringing as the news got around his family in the UK and Ghana. Esther lay with her hands on her belly. She had put up with barbed comments from John's mother for years about the lack of a grandchild and now she was giving them what they wanted.

As a single tear rolled down her cheek, Esther wondered what this would mean for the future of her and John and their child. She could imagine that his mother, in particular, would try to take over and if they were going to have to rely on her for childcare because Esther was working, she could see herself being pushed to the sidelines of her baby's life. Now in the quiet of her bedroom, she repeated a saying to herself that goes:

Love is not emotions
Love is a choice.
It does not need a reason.
Love is a force generated by a decision.
Love is an act of the will.
Love is debt you owe.
Love is a law. Which has nothing to do with your feelings.
Love is not a gift. It's the fruit of the spirit. Either it is in you by God's grace or you don't have it.
Understanding love will help you to use it.
Love is caring, anticipating a need and meeting it.

They were words that Esther intended to live her life by with her baby and with John. This was going to be their new start. Despite his family, she could feel it.

Esther was entering the final critical stages of her degree. John had finished his and was now teaching at the university so Esther could finally give up her nursing. It was a huge relief financially and it gave Esther hope for the future. Ruth was delighted that her daughter was expecting but worried that she had so much on her plate. Levi was hoping for a boy that he could teach to play football!

Esther was in turmoil with mixed feelings. She had loved nursing and she knew that she had made a difference to countless people's lives. She was still in touch with Malaya and Huda who were thriving under the care of their Saudi saviours. When she could, Esther still volunteered at the hospice and comforted herself that she could continue to do that. It was the end of an era. Now she was starting a new life, qualified at last and able to work towards making a difference to people's lives in a bigger way at the grass root level.

Moreover, she would be a mother responsible for another human being, shaping the way they grew and the way that they developed and formed their personality. It was a daunting responsibility. But it was a responsibility that Esther was ready to take on wholeheartedly. She already loved the child inside her with an intensity that she had never thought possible and she knew that she would be the best mother she could.

Now that she was not working, Esther threw herself into her studies and the final push worked well for her. As her morning sickness faded, she concentrated on preparing for her final exams and was rewarded with an honours degree.

It was a proud moment and as she mounted the stage to receive her degree from London City university she could see her mother dabbing at her eyes. Levi was whooping wildly. John and his family were also there.

John smiled at her proudly but the rest of his family made it quite clear from the expressions on their faces that they were far from impressed.

Esther had already been offered a job as a human rights lawyer (in combination with international corporate governance and financial law) with Humanity First, a charity that dealt chiefly with the Middle East. This was something that Esther was passionate about and she could not wait to take up her position.

Even the fact that she was expecting did not put off her potential employers. They could see the passion that Esther had for the work that they did. Her experience in Saudi Arabia with Malaya was also something that they valued. They agreed that Esther would work from home when her baby was born with just one day a week in the office. Her workload would be kept minimal to begin with and she was introduced to a charming man, Chris Walker who was also a lawyer with many years of experience in the human rights field.

As her baby's birth approached, Esther felt happier than she had in years. John was kind and considerate of her and even her mother in law seemed to be softening, perhaps realising that she needed to be that way if she was going to be as involved in her grandchild's life as she wanted to be.

They were moving to a bigger garden flat as well, and even though they would now have to pay full rent, they could afford it and Esther loved the extra room that they had, the baby would have a room that overlooked the small garden at the back. Esther loved to watch the birds on the feeders that she put out for them.

Back from Saudi for a visit, Lizzie helped Esther to decorate the baby's nursery.

"Do you know what you are having?"

"No, they offered to say at my scan, but John and I wanted it to be a surprise."

"We did the same, do you have a preference, boy or girl?"

"Well I know that John would love to have a son, it's a kind of African male thing, but as long as it has ten fingers and toes I really don't mind." Esther said.

"I love this colour!" Lizzie said, dabbing the end of her paintbrush on Esther's nose, "It really suits you!"

Esther laughed and dabbed Lizzie back.

"What's going on here then?" It was John. "I thought you girls were decorating the nursery, not each other!" He smiled his most charming smile, the one that he reserved for attractive ladies. Lizzie smiled back.

"Well you better go and put the kettle on or we might start decorating you too!" She laughed.

John backed out of the nursery, his hands in the air.

"I surrender!" He said, "Hot chocolate all round?"

"Yes please," the girls chorused.

"You've got a good un there Esther." Lizzie said, "And so handsome. If I wasn't happily married…"

Esther smiled. If only Lizzie knew the whole story.

Finally, the baby was ready to come into the world. At three in the morning Esther woke up with a start, her waters had broken. As the pains began and took her breath away, John rushed her to hospital and Esther prayed.

I entrust my spirit into your hand. Rescue me Lord, for you are a faithful God. (Psalm 31:5)

Chapter Eleven

New Life and New Hope

The birth was difficult and long and Esther prayed for strength. The midwives could not recall a more serene labouring woman or one who so politely refused anything but the most basic pain relief. Some few hours after they arrived in the hospital, John's family arrived. Esther heard them talking to John in the corridor. She breathed even more deeply, she could not let anything distract her from the miracle that was about to happen.

When John came back into the room she asked.

"Is mum here yet?"

John did not reply.

"John, you did call her didn't you?"

"I'll do that right now, baby." He said reaching for his phone.

Esther bit her lip. She could not believe he hadn't let her mother know that she had gone into labour.

"When she arrives, can you make sure that she comes in here right away please?" Esther asked as another powerful contraction gripped her.

"Ok baby, and my mum too?"

"No!" Esther hissed through teeth clenched against the pain.

As the contraction subsided she breathed deeply. "John please, I am not an exhibit, I need my mum, and you. No-one else."

"Ok, baby, Ok," John kissed her head as Ruth answered the phone to him.

Ruth was at the hospital in half an hour and at Esther's side. With her mother holding one hand and John the other, Esther felt blessed. The pain came over her in waves but she prayed and breathed and finally with a last push her baby was born. "Congratulations, it's a boy!" The midwife said placing her tiny son on Esther's chest.

Looking down at the serene face of her son, Esther felt a wave of love come over her that took her breath away. John and Ruth were crying, and John was kissing her face while he put out a tentative finger to trace the side of his sons face. The infant opened his eyes and stared straight at Esther's. Esther's breath caught in her throat as she looked down at her perfect son, who seemed to look straight into her soul.

Taking her mother's and John's hands, Esther repeated a prayer she had said many times to herself through her pregnancy.

Father God, we come before you, the Creator of the Universe, the Creator of our child.

We bless you and praise you for the works of your hand. O God, you are mighty and full of wisdom. You have sent forth your Spirit and have created our son.

And we agree with you that he will change the face of the earth, as he changes the world of each of us who loves him.

We thank you that you have given life to our son and we welcome him. We speak to him and tell him he is loved and supported on his journey.

We speak to him and tell him of the wondrous deeds of her Creator.

Son, the God of all Creation has formed your inward parts; He has woven you in your mother's womb.

We give thanks to God for you are fearfully and wonderfully made; wonderful are God's works and your soul knows it very well.

Your frame was not hidden from God when you were made in secret, and skilfully wrought in the depths of the earth.

God's eyes have seen your unformed substance and in God's book is written all the days that have been ordained for you, when as yet there has not been one of them.

Father God has clothed you with skin and flesh and knitted you together with bones and sinews.

He has granted you life and loving kindness. God's care is preserving your spirit. The Lord who made you and formed you in the womb will help you. Do not fear.

"Amen," they all said together.

Outside, the midwife had brought the happy news to the waiting family and the door of the delivery room burst open as John's mother and sisters all stampeded towards the bed.

Esther gathered her son to her instinctively, protecting him. But John took him gently from her arms and showed him proudly to his mother and sisters.

His mother all but snatched the child from her son and was about to take him out to meet the rest of the family when Esther put her hand on John's arm, her eyes silently pleading with him.

John moved quickly. He stood between his mother and the door.

"Mum, give him back to me, please." He said firmly and his mother stopped in her tracks, unaccustomed to being spoken to in such a way by her son.

"But John we just wanted..."

John held out his hands and his mother handed the tiny bundle over and John placed him gently back in Esther's arms.

Turning to his mother he said, "All in good time, mummy, I don't think that Esther is ready to be separated from him just yet."

Esther looked up at him, tears of pride and gratitude shining in her eyes. This was going to be their new start, she could feel it. It was the first time that she had seen him stand up to his mother for her. Her heart swelled with pride and hope. They were going to be all right.

Esther's hopes were short lived. Almost as soon as they got back from the hospital, a huge row started about what their son should be named. John's family, with him as their mouthpiece, had already decided on the names that their newest prince would be called. Some of those names were traditional Ghanaian names that would have been great for a child growing up in Accra, but not so much for a boy whose home was going to be London.

Esther wondered if the desire for the traditional names could have been a regret John's parents felt that they had chosen very Western names for their own children. Whatever the idea that was behind it, on the subject of her precious son's name, Esther was not going to allow anyone to bully her.

To her dismay, their son's first few weeks of life were lived to the soundtrack of her and John arguing over the names that he should be called. Esther was definitely in favour of a biblical name for her son and eventually she and John came to an agreement. Their son was to be called Daniel Frederick Sarkodie Sanderson. Naturally John's family disapproved. There was no doubt that they thought Esther was not good enough for their son and certainly not good enough to mother the new prince of the dynasty.

Juggling motherhood with her new job and continued study was harder than Esther had ever thought it would be. She wanted so much to be a full time mum but she had fought too hard and for too long to let her dream career drift away.

At work, Chris Walker was kind and understanding and she found herself relaxing in his company and looking forward to seeing him when she went in whenever she reported. As she found her feet, she was aware that he was carrying her, helping her much more than she could ever had imagined possible, and she was so grateful for it.

When she was at home with Daniel, Esther loved every minute of their time together. She would sit and just watch him sleep and think how lucky she was. In the periphery of her consciousness, she was aware of something new in John. He was jealous of the time that she spent caring for Daniel.

John was jealous of his own son! Esther, who had made what effort she could to keep up with things in the house before her son's birth now made no effort to tidy up after John. Every moment that he had she spent with her son. Ruth was a frequent visitor. Together they resisted the almost overwhelming pressure from her in-laws to let them have Daniel. Ruth had finally stopped working and was delighted to look after her grandson. Mother and daughter would dodge John's family by spiriting Daniel to Ruth's house.

During weekends when she and John would visit his family, Daniel would be whisked away at the front door and only be handed back when Esther left. She could not, would not, let them take over.

John had his nose well and truly put out of joint by Esther's new busy life caring for their son, writing her thesis and working at her job. He stayed out late into the night, going to nightclubs and coming back drunk and smelling of perfume. Esther ignored it and ignored the fact that he would not come to bed until he thought that she was asleep, that he barely communicated with her at all and bothered with Daniel only when it suited him.

Lizzie was visiting and eager to meet Daniel. She came to the flat, laden with gifts for the new arrival, and arrived right in the heat of an argument. Although they stopped rowing as soon as she arrived, Lizzie could feel the atmosphere and did not miss the fact that barely acknowledging her, John threw on his coat, and slammed out of the flat with such force that the windows rattled.

"Hey Esther, what's up?" Lizzie put her arm around her friend, dropping Daniel's presents on the couch.

Esther was mortified. She was so envious of how happy Lizzie and Adam were together and she childishly wanted her friend to think that she and John were just as happy. She had never told Lizzie the difficulties that she and John had, but now it all came pouring out. As Esther told Lizzie what her life had been with John, her friends face expressed, first shock and then anger and finally sorrow as the two sat and cried together.

"What are you going to do Esther?" Lizzie wiped her eyes.

"I don't know. We're in the middle of buying this place. It's such a mess." Esther sobbed.

"What about your mum, what does she say?" Lizzie asked.

"I don't tell her the half of it." Esther said. "She would only worry and her life is, at last, a bit easier. She's stopped work and she has time for herself and time to stand getting freezing cold at Levi's football matches. I want her to be relaxed and not to worry about me. Now that I am a mother myself, it makes me appreciate, even more, the sacrifices that she made for Levi and me when we were growing up. I know that I had a lot put on me as a child, but I am so grateful that she held it all together for us."

"Confide in her Esther," Lizzie said, "You can't go through this alone and you are going to need her support if the worst comes to the worst."

Hearing Lizzie speak so frankly, Esther felt a coldness start in the pit of her stomach and spread through her body until she began to shiver. It was as though saying it out loud suddenly made it very real. She and John might split up. It was something that she dreaded, and now that they had Daniel it was even more unimaginable.

She closed her eyes imagining the furore there would be with John's family. She already has a suspicion that John was cooking something up with them, or at least with his sister Cheryl as he was spending more and more time with her and she was becoming an almost permanent fixture in the flat, on the pretext of helping John with Daniel, when Esther was not home.

If Esther came home while the brother and sister were there, they would immediately stop talking and John would snap the top of the laptop down, obviously keen that Esther did not see what they were doing.

Esther knew that something was going on but she was focused on Daniel and she just could not be bothered with John and his nonsense anymore. It suited her just fine that Cheryl would scuttle off as soon as she came home.

After Lizzie had gone, Esther sat for a long time in the rocking chair in Daniel's room, cradling her sleeping son on her lap. As the room became dark she thought about what her future would be if she and John split up. Now that she was qualified and gaining experience she was confident that she could earn a decent living that would keep them both.

But what revenge would his family exact? Esther knew that they would be fighting tooth and nail for their son, whatever the rights and wrongs of the situation. She held Daniel tighter. Esther knew that if she and John did split there would be many difficult months and even years ahead. But she had her faith to uphold her. She had that. The longer she knew John the more she thought he was paying little more than lip service to his faith. That made her sad. She sat and recited verses that had given her strength through her life.

Ask and it will be given to you; seek and you will find; knock and the door will be opened to you. (Matthew 7:7)

In life if you want the blessings and promises of God, you should ask, you should seek, you should knock or you will be waiting, praying and crying and even wondering why me?

But I want to let you know: the things you are going through are preparing you for what you asked for -your hearts desire. Your desires won't come just like that: Look at the rain that turns into a storm. Then comes the rainbow and finally the sun will shine. That's how it is! You will be a baby turning into a toddler then a teenager and finally a man or woman. All this will happen gradually, for the Lord our God didn't make the world in one day! Lets us endure in patience and faith .

Blessed is the man who perseveres under trial, because when he has stood the test, he will receive the crown of life that God has promised to those who love him. (James 1:12)

The familiar words comforted Esther; she knew that she was never alone but that God was her constant companion. He would give her the strength that she needed.

It had felt good to get it off her chest to her friend and Esther decided that it was time to confide in her mother. She was going with her mother to watch Levi play in his first selection for the main team and it would be the first time little Daniel had been out to an event. Esther had been quite relieved when John said that he could not come. It would give her the chance to speak to her mother. She hoped that being at the match might help to distract her from the sadness of what she had to tell her. But Esther would have to choose her moment.

The day of Levi's first team game dawned bright and Esther wrapped Daniel up warmly for his first visit to the Arsenal stadium. She was nervous and butterflies swirled disconcertingly in her stomach. She was so proud of her brother but also dreading the conversation that she knew that she had to have with her. As relatives of a player they were shown to a box with other players' families, some of whom Esther recognised as WAGS from glossy magazines and newspapers. It was quite overwhelming. They saw Levi briefly before the match and kissed him for luck.

Tucked away in the corner of the relatives box, Esther felt that the general chatter drowned her out sufficiently that she could talk to her mother without being overheard. Out on the pitch Levi was doing well and had already set up two goals for his strikers. The crowd was going mad and a sea of red and white scarves rippled around the stadium like waves.

Ruth sat, her hands clasped in front of her mouth, a huge smile on her face. "Go on Levi, go on son!" She whispered as Levi ran down the left wing again, the ball expertly controlled at the tip of his boots. As he turned towards the centre of the pitch ready to pass to his centre forward, an opposing player, desperate to stop a third goal slid hard into Levi, whipping his legs from under him.

The referee was quick to react blowing his whistle for a foul. But Levi was on the ground, his screams of agony audible even through the glass of the relatives box. Esther felt herself go stone cold as her eyes went to the TV screen in the box that had zoomed in on her brother. As it went in for a close up it cut away instantly but not before Esther had seen the brilliant white of her brothers' shin bone protruding through his skin. There were gasps of horror around the stadium and one of the players closest to Levi threw up on the pitch.

The paramedics were on the pitch now and a screen had been put up around Levi. Next, to her Esther could hear her mother saying softly

"No, no, no, please God, no."

On shaking legs, Esther and her mother left the box with sympathetic eyes following them. The ambulance had already taken Levi away but they were told he was going to St Thomas', the hospital that Esther had worked at some time back.

Esther helped her mother into a taxi and they travelled in silence to the hospital. Even baby Daniel seemed to be in shock, as his bright eyes stared into his mothers, as if he sensed that something was wrong.

At the hospital Esther quickly changed her son's nappy and joined her mother in the relative's room while they waited for news of Levi who had been taken straight to theatre. As Esther held her son to the breast and watched him feed, her mother stroked the child's cheek. It was as though they needed something to focus on, however temporary.

When the news finally came it was not good. Levi had suffered a compound break to his leg and was having plates fitted. So severe was the injury that the repair would mean his right leg would always be slightly shorter than his left. He would not be able to play professional football again.

Chapter Twelve
The downward spiral

In the weeks that followed Levi's accident, Esther's problems were temporarily forgotten. In fact, she and John worked together to help her devastated brother. He was getting the best of treatment, paid for by Arsenal, but his spirit was broken. From the time that he could first kick a ball, he had had no other dream; he wanted to be a professional footballer. Now that was not going to be possible. No matter how he wheedled the medical staff to give him even the tiniest crumb of hope that the situation might change, they stood firm by their prognosis. He would never play football professionally again.

Levi sank into deep depression and John spent every moment that he could with the boy, trying to encourage him in his recovery and trying to show him that there could be a future without football. Esther was glad now that she had said nothing to her mother about her marriage now, maybe, just maybe they would be all right. The concern John showed to Levi and the support he was to her and her mother gave her a glimpse of the John with whom she had fallen in love.

At home, however, things were still tense. John was still staying out late at night and being very secretive around his laptop and with his meetings with Cheryl. He was proud of their son Daniel but still seemed to resent the amount of time that Esther had to devote to him. Esther pushed their problems to the back of her mind as she worked and studied hard and cared for Daniel whilst leaving enough time to see Levi and support her mother. Levi was home from hospital and Esther hoped that having Daniel around would cheer him up, and it did seem to, at least.

Some months later on a hot June day, Esther was pushing Daniel in his buggy through the shopping street near the flat when a neighbour of John's family stopped her.

"Let me see that little prince!" She cooed peering in at Daniel who smiled cheerfully at her. "We don't see him around at Abena's very much!"

Esther smiled.

"Well, you now how it is, we are all so busy."

"Well, certainly John is." The woman said, throwing out a teasing line and waiting for Esther to bite.

Despite herself, Esther bit.

"Oh, how do you mean?"

Delighted that Esther had taken the bait the woman said.

"Well, I was surprised that you weren't involved in the shop. It seems to me that something like that should be more a husband and wife thing rather than a brother and sister thing."

Esther felt herself reeling and fought to disguise her shock from this woman who was obviously on a mission to stir up trouble.

"Have you seen it yet?" The woman was obviously determined and took Esther by the arm propelling her along the street until they came to a stop in front of a shop with a newly painted sign that read -

John and Cheryl Interiors

Cheryl felt her mouth drop open and quickly closed it aware that the nosy neighbour was watching her every move like a hawk hovering over a field mouse. Esther's eyes darted over the items that she could see in the window and the shop interior behind and she could tell immediately that what she could see represented thousands of pounds worth of stock.

Esther's mind was whirling. Where had they got the money from? Feeling an icy fist of fear grip her stomach and ignoring the nosy neighbour, she turned Daniel's buggy around and almost ran to the building society. With shaking fingers, she keyed in her pin number and a figure popped up on screen.

John had all but emptied their savings.

At their flat, Esther waited for John to come home. She tried to calm herself down and busied herself with bathing Daniel and putting him to bed. Daniel was fractious and irritated and Esther wondered if her agitation was affecting him. When she heard John's key in the door, the few butterflies that had been swirling in her stomach turned into a swarm.

When she confronted him, John was unapologetic.

"Esther, you are so controlling, always wanting to know what I'm doing, so what if I am trying to make a future for us and Daniel? What's so bad about that?"

"What's so bad is that we are supposed to be husband and wife and we are not supposed to have secrets from each other, especially a secret as big as this." Esther fought to hold back her tears. The fact that John could get as far as opening a shop with his sister that Esther knew nothing about said a lot about the sate of their marriage.

John snorted. "Well, not so much husband and wife as mother and child. You only have time for Daniel and your work and study. If you don't care about me, why should I care what you think about my business?"

"Because, John, you've all but emptied our savings to do it! That was mostly money that I saved in Saudi, you had no right to use it without consulting me!"

"I am your husband, what's yours is mine, or have you forgotten your wedding vows?" John thundered and from his nursery, Daniel began to cry, woken by John's raised voice.

"All right, John we'll talk about this later, I don't want Daniel to sense an atmosphere." Esther said, her voice shaking.

"Daniel, Daniel, Daniel. It's all you can think about!" John said sarcastically, and Esther turned on him.

"And he should be all you can think about too, if you were any kind of a father!" Esther shouted, but John had already slammed out of the door.

Esther hurried to Daniel. The child was crying, tears rolling down his face and as she sat down in the rocking chair, Esther began to cry too.

She did not want to make it all about money. The truth was she felt betrayed by John because he had not spoken to her, and not only that, he had taken great pains to hide what he was doing from her. Esther thought of a saying that she had heard.

Money only impresses lazy girls. When she works hard a man with money is a bonus not a ladder to upgrade.

And that was how she had always looked at things. John had next to nothing when they met; he had not been working long and was irresponsible with his money. Esther was the one with money and she had never held that over him, until now.

That Sunday they attended church. They had not spoken since their argument at the beginning of the week, but John was very keen on keeping up appearances, so they walked in silence to the church. Esther was miserable. She knelt and prayed.

"Lord do you know what? Even in all my problems, I am going to love and serve you, all the days of my life. I don't care about my difficulties, I just want to be that person that you want me to be. I will concentrate on my love for you and let you lift the burden from me. You will make me free from fear."

Esther felt peace descend on her and she immediately relaxed into the service. The peace she felt, however, was short-lived.

John had been asked to give a talk about success and ambition that tied in with the Bible reading of the day and proudly mentioned the business he and Cheryl were running. Things went from bad to worse as the congregation gathered on the pavement outside the church after the service.

The nosy neighbour who had stopped Esther in the high street was joined by other members of the congregation eager to ask Esther what she thought of her husband and sister going into business together. Esther pasted a smile on her face and acted as though she had known about it all the time, muttering things like.

"Oh yes I am sure they are going to be a great success."
And
"Well Cheryl is so artistic and John is so good with numbers, they are bound to succeed."

Esther was aware of eyes on her waiting for her to

show any sign of martial discord over her husband and sister in law's business venture.

"But it's strange that your husband and his sister, rather than you and he are going into business." One particularly persistent enquirer asked.

"Oh my goodness, with Daniel my work and my study I have no time for anything else," Esther said with a laugh that even to her, sounded false. She could see John looking at her but she did not meet his gaze.

The next week, while Esther was with her mother, Ruth mentioned the shop.

"You kept that quiet, Esther!"

"I didn't know," Esther said, her voice flat.

"Of course you knew!" Ruth said.

"I didn't mum, just like I didn't know he was going to all but empty our savings account to do it."

Ruth looked at Esther. She could see that her daughter was upset, but she couldn't understand why.

"Well you must be proud of him."

"No I'm not! I'm angry with him for taking the money without asking me." Esther could hear the anger rising in her own voice.

"Now then Esther," Ruth said, "When you are married you share everything and I don't really think that getting angry with John for trying to make a future for you is a good thing."

"I provided a future for him by financing us through his studies, how much more does he expect of me?"

"Esther," Ruth's tone was sharp now. "You have to stop thinking about the money as yours alone, it is something that is for the family, not just for you!"

"Mum you don't understand!" Esther was in tears now. "He's secretive and if he is thinking of anything it is Cheryl and his family not me and Daniel."

"No, I'm sorry, Esther, this will not do! "I know that Abena has criticised you before for not understanding your role as a wife, and I am beginning to think she has a point!"

Esther gasped. Grabbing Daniel, she slammed out of her mother's house. So much for confiding in her mother about her problems, she appeared to love John more than her own daughter. She was certainly taking his side.

Esther was at her lowest ebb. She went through the motions of work and study and Chris Walker proved himself to be a good friend. Esther was aware that he was carrying her at work and she hated it. She had always been a hard worker but her life seemed to be unravelling and she had no choice but to lean on her colleague and friend.

Daniel was coming up to his first birthday. As low as she was feeling, Esther was determined to make it a special day for her son. For the first time in a long time, she opened a discussion with John about the arrangements for the party. John waved his hand at her dismissively.

"Esther, I am far too busy to be involved with a party for a kid who won't even know what is going on."

Esther was speechless; she could barely believe what John was saying. What father did not get excited about his son's first birthday party? Fighting back the tears, Esther said nothing and took comfort, as usual, in the inspiration sayings that so often comforted her.

What a tragedy – you chose to become a slave to bitterness and almost everything that falls under the umbrella of hate. Being hurt again consumes you. It's a shame you let one person's bad choice have such power over you. It's a shame to let your experiences keep you from one of the greatest human experiences: to love and be loved in the right way.

Esther knew that she was in danger of becoming bitter and she was determined to do everything she could to avoid that. Esther carried on with the arrangements for Daniel's birthday. Lizzie was home on a visit and she and Tessa helped too, packing little goodie bags for the children who would be coming and baking a birthday cake and cupcakes and making bowls of raspberry jelly.

Arriving home as the girls were finishing up on the dining table with the goodie bags, Lizzie's face changed the minute she saw John.

Esther had told her some of what was going on but aware of how awkward it would be if Lizzie absolutely hated John, she had held back. Lizzie had been understanding of the fact that she had not told her mother and had been shocked at the change in the once cheeky, full of life Levi. Esther had made a lot of the fact that John had been so good with Levi and for that Lizzie was pleased. But the change in her friend was obvious too. Esther had lost weight and had a haunted look in her eyes.

Lizzie was worried about her friend. John might be good with Levi but one thing for sure was that he was not good for Esther. Lizzie had been shocked to hear about the shop and although Esther tried to make light of it, she could tell that it had shaken her friend deeply. Lizzie knew how hard Esther had worked for the money she had saved while working in the Saudi Kingdom and her heart broke for her friend. Her own marriage to Adam was great and they were friends as well as husband and wife. She wished that Esther could have that too.

To avoid saying anything that would worsen the situation, Lizzie left with Tessa.

Seeing the goodie bags on the table, John picked one up and threw it down again. "So have you involved my sisters in this *party of the century?*" John said sarcastically.

"No I haven't, I assumed they would share your view of a birthday party for a one year old."

"You know what Esther?" He shouted, "I am so sick of the way that you try to be so clever. You are not clever, you are rude and ungrateful and you only ever think of yourself. My sisters are very hurt that you did not ask them to be involved."

Esther felt her hackles rise.

"If they really do want to be involved, let them make a salad. Tell them that if you want, but I'm not going to! In any case I thought Cheryl at least would be too busy with your new business venture." She shouted back.

"Oh, I wondered how long it would be before you brought that up!" John laughed a cold laugh.

"You just can't bear anyone doing something that you re not involved with. You are a complete control freak!"

"Me?" Esther said, "If I was I would have left you long ago. No one controls you John, you do exactly what you want and you don't give a damn about anyone else. You are a user and a taker." Esther shocked herself with the ferocity of her outburst. John was obviously shocked too. He stared at her for a moment, and then crossed to the door. As he stood with his hand on the door handle, he said in a low menacing voice,

"You would have left me long ago, would you? Well here's the door," he threw the door open, "Go ahead!"

Esther sat down, her head in her hands.

"Don't worry, I'll save you the trouble, I'm out of here. I'll come back for my stuff later." And John was gone.

Esther fell to her knees in the middle of the lounge and prayed.

Heavenly Father, I come before you today with a heavy heart; my marriage is in trouble, and I need your help. Make changes in my spouse's heart. Make us compatible again, and bring us closer together. Fill us with your love and give us the strength to love one another, care for one another, and fulfill your destiny for us.

Show us the harm caused by careless words, and the pain caused by emotional distance. Bring us together, like we once were. Show us how to love one another again.

Heal the division between us. If it is thy will, make us one again.

In your name I pray, Amen.

Esther was crying as she prayed over and over again. In her heart she hoped that her prayer would be answered but in her mind she was afraid that things might have gone too far. In the quiet of the flat that seemed to echo with the angry words they had shouted at each other, Esther cried. She had never felt so alone; her God was her only comfort now.

John's family welcomed him home like a returning hero. It seemed to Esther that they had been waiting for this day since John and she had got married. Extra food was fetched and a homecoming feast cooked for the returning prince. His family sympathised with their son. They had known for a long time that Esther was not a suitable wife; she was too headstrong, too managing and not subservient enough. They felt she had led their son into a merry dance, and they were very glad he was home again where he would be appreciated.

John's family put the word out that Daniel's party was cancelled, although some people did not get the word and arrived at the flat finding Esther completely unprepared. She called Lizzie and her friend turned up within half an hour to save the day. In the end, it was a small muted affair but one that Daniel seemed to enjoy nonetheless.

For Esther though, it was the calm before a huge storm that was heading fast in her direction.

Chapter Thirteen

Rock Bottom

Esther was devastated. She felt as though she did not have a friend in this world. A terrible depression descended on her, not helped by her mother's constant insistence that Esther apologise to John and make everything right.

Esther was hurt that her mother seemed to be taking John's side and she found herself in a bitter argument with her.

"Esther you have to back down! You have a child, you have to do whatever you can to make this right, he is your husband, its up to you to keep your marriage together."

"Oh yes, just like you did?" Esther snapped back and was immediately sorry that she had been so cruel. Her mother's face registered her deep hurt; Esther might as well have slapped her.

"All right Esther," Ruth said quietly. "Since you seem intent on ruining your life and Daniel's too, you go ahead. I have enough to worry about with Levi." Ruth wiped her hands together in an exaggerated 'washing my hands off you' gesture.

Esther cried all the way back to the flat. As she walked through the high street, she saw that John and Cheryl's shop now had sale stickers all over the items in the window. Clearly things were not going well. It was just another thing for her to worry about. She had never felt so low.

When Esther got back to the flat, John was waiting for her. He was sitting in the lounge and she did not immediately realise that he was there. He had not put the light on, or the TV. He was sitting in the semi-dark room, his arms resting along the arms of the chair and his face set in an uncompromising forward stare. He did not acknowledge Esther or Daniel and Esther hurried to the bedroom to put Daniel in his cot. He was asleep and she hoped he would stay that way.

When she came back to the lounge, John was standing at the window, his back to her. He still had his coat on.

"What do you want John?" Esther said.

"I've come around to talk to you."

"You mean your mother and father told you to come around and talk to me," Esther said bitterly.

Now John swung around.

"You are a total bitch Esther, I don't know what I ever saw in you. You have never liked my family and they have been nothing but kindness to you, you are a total ungrateful bitch!"

Esther gasped.

"Your family have *never* been kind to me. They made no secret of the fact that they never thought I was good enough for their precious son. You are such a pathetic mummy's boy, you always took their side over mine!"

"Sides, sides! That's all you ever bleat on and you are so stupid that you don't even realise that it's not about sides. How immature can you be? You're like a spoiled brat who always wants her own way!"

"John you know that's not true! I have always worked hard for everything. I never had anything handed to me on a plate, like you did." They stood opposite each other, the anger in the room so thick it could be cut with a knife.

Esther wanted to say 'How have we got here? We used to be so much in love.' But she knew that it was much too late for that now. Their marriage was in its death throes and the pain of that was almost physical. Looking at John, however, she could see the hate in his eyes. He had not just fallen out of love with her – he hated her.

"What do you want John?" Esther repeated, her voice choked with tears that she absolutely refused to shed in front of John.

"Well, as I said, I wanted to talk to you, but I can see that is a waste of time!" He shouted.

Esther wanted to stop and talk, wanted so much to save her marriage but she could not let him walk over her anymore. She did not trust him and she could see that he hated her. There was nothing more to say.

John walked into the bedroom they had shared and threw some of his stuff into a case. Esther was fighting a battle with herself.

"John!" She said bursting into tears, hating herself for her weakness.

"John!"

He turned to look at her. "Please!" She croaked.

"Get out of my way! God you're pathetic Esther, I don't know what I ever saw in you! John shoved her to one side and Esther overbalanced, falling onto the floor beside the bed. She yelped in pain as her head hit the bedside table.

John did not give her a backward glance. Moments later, the front door slammed.

It was dark now and Esther lay beside the bed, curled into a foetal position, deep sobs wracking her body. She touched her fingers to her head and felt the sticky warmth of blood. She didn't care. The superficial wound on her head was nothing compared to the gaping wound in her heart. She closed here eyes tight and began to pray.

Grant unto me, Almighty God, in all times of sore distress, the comfort of the forgiveness of my sins. In time of darkness give me blessed hope, in time of sickness of body give me quiet courage; and when the heart is bowed down, and the soul is very heavy, and life is a burden, and pleasure a weariness, and the sun is too bright, and life too mirthful, then may that Spirit, the Spirit of the Comforter, come upon me, and after our darkness may there be the clear shining of the heavenly light; that so, being uplifted again by Thy mercy, I may pass on through this our mortal life with quiet courage, patient hope, and unshaken trust, hoping through Thy loving-kindness and tender mercy to be delivered from death into the large life of the eternal years. Hear me of Thy mercy, through Jesus Christ our Lord – Amen.

Esther repeated the prayer that she knew by heart over and over again and gradually she became calm. Her heart ached and she had started to shake with cold as she lay on the floor. Dragging herself up, Esther walked to the bathroom. The light, when she turned it on, hurt her eyes after so long in the darkness. She inspected the cut on her head.

The blood had dried but was little more than a scratch. Esther dampened a flannel and dabbed at the dry blood. As she rinsed the cloth off under the tap, a thin stream of watery blood snaked its way down the drain. Esther stared until the water ran clear.

Her limbs felt heavy as she walked into the lounge. She sat in the darkness, only the light from the street lamps casting eerie shafts of light where they shone in through the window. Esther realised that she was listening for John's key in the lock. She sobbed quietly now and she prayed again. This time the only prayer she could remember was the first prayer that she had ever learned – The Lord's Prayer.

Esther felt a sense of calm descend on her, but it was short-lived. Her shoulders shook as she started to cry again. She heard Daniel whimpering and went through to see if he was all right. The little boy was awake and staring up at her, smiling. Esther scooped him out of his cot and sat in the rocking chair with him, kissing his face. His eyes began to close, flying open for a second as one of her tears landed on his cheek, but before long he was asleep.

In Esther's mind, her life with John played out like a movie; the day that they met, the times that they had studied the Bible together. She remembered the magical weekend in Plymouth and the day that John had proposed. Esther could see the leaves swirling in the wind around them and hear their laughter.

What had happened? What was going to happen? Esther put Daniel back in his cot and waked back to the lounge. As she walked, her bare foot trod on something sharp. She reached down. She had trodden on John's keys. He was not coming back.

John's family had decided that as there was a child involved, they would have to get the family priest involved. One by one the sisters and the parents came to the flat to talk to Esther. Cheryl, in particular, was merciless.

"You see, what I don't understand Esther is how you can be so cruel to John?"

Esther was speechless.

"All he wants is to make a success of things for you and

Daniel, but you are fighting him all the way!"

"Cheryl," Esther tried to keep calm. "I am not fighting. I certainly do not want us to split up, I've done my best but John is selfish and secretive and more interested in anything else than me and Daniel."

"Wow!" Cheryl said. "John told us what a vicious cow you could be, and I didn't believe him, but now I see what he means. No wonder he can't stand to be around you!"

"Cheryl, what John tells you is not necessarily what happens." Esther fought to keep cool.

"Esther! Don't you think that we all have problems in our marriages? But those of us who are truly committed to being a wife make an effort, we don't whine all the time about what we want and what our husband should do for us. We sacrifice and make the marriage work. How can you continue to be such a bitch when John has done so much for you?"

Now Esther could not control herself any longer.

"So much for me?" She squeaked. "Oh you must mean how he spent all my money on the shop that he opened with you and now looks like it's going out of business? Or maybe you mean how he complains all the time about how much time I spend caring for our son? Or did you mean the time that she spends in nightclubs and chatting up other women?"

Cheryl was shaking her head.

"I never took you for a liar, Esther, but I can see that what John has been telling us is right. You are a 'class A' bitch and a selfish cow and what's worse is that you can't see it!"

Esther stood up and opened the front door. Cheryl, her mouth open in shock left the flat and Esther slammed the door hard behind her. It was pointless talking to anyone from John's family. They were going to take his side and they would never believe her over their precious prince.

Cheryl's visit was not the last and over the weeks that followed Esther put up with a barrage of insults and verbal attacks from various members of John's family.

"You never were good enough for our John," his mother spat at her. "Your poor mother, she must be so ashamed!"

Even John's father got in on the act. He sat opposite Esther shaking his head.

"Esther, you have got it all so wrong. You are not a wife; you are just a woman who wants everything your own way. You are a disgrace and if I had been unlucky enough to marry someone like you, I would not even have lasted as long as John has."

Even her own mother was leaning hard on Esther to try and make things right. Esther could tell that Ruth did not believe what she was hearing about her son in law and Esther felt more and more isolated. She knew that her life was falling apart and she was barely able to function at work. Her study was suffering too and it was as much as she could do to go through the motions of life every day.

Next, John's family, in a move that was common in African culture where a marriage was in trouble, called on their pastor to mediate. Esther felt herself sink further into depression. There was no point in the pastor intervening; she knew that it was just prolonging the agony, and it would be horrible to have to 'wash her dirty linen in public.'

But John, playing the dutiful victim, agreed to it and she looked like the difficult one by saying that she was not keen to it. Esther knew that the reason that her marriage had not succeeded was because John's family had never liked her. They had such a strong influence over him that anyone that they did not approve of would never stand a chance. Esther had been tolerated at best, but she knew now that the marriage had little chance of success.

With her mother looking after Daniel, Esther went to church. It was quiet inside the building and she was the only person in there. She prayed quietly as tears coursed down her face. She was 24 years old, she had given five years to a man whom she doubted now had ever loved her. John had taken her innocence, taken her heart and her trust and taken her money. He was even indifferent towards their son, except when it suited him or when he was showing off for the benefit of other people and playing the doting father.

Now Esther wondered what her life had become. How had she ended up with a failed marriage and was now about to become a single mother before she was even 25? Why had God not helped her to save her marriage? Why had God let John walk away? As she prayed some words popped into her mind.

The reason that God allowed him to walk away was because you prayed for a good man, and he was not a good man.

Esther took a deep breath. She felt the hand of God on her and she straightened her back. She had a son, she had Daniel and she would stay strong for him.

Esther returned to work, ignoring her mother's disapproving look as she dropped Daniel off. Chris was delighted to see her. Esther was pleased to see him too. Esther brought Chris up to date with what was going on and she could see the look of concern on his face as she described the almost daily verbal abuse she was suffering from John and his family, and the fact that all her savings were gone, taken by John before she had a chance to cancel the joint account and set up one on her own.

"Oh Esther, I'm so sorry, you've been having a really tough time. Is there anything I can do?"

"Just seeing your friendly face is a great pick me up," Esther smiled. "Working will be a good distraction."

At home there were other problems to overcome. She and John had been buying the flat in which they lived. His cousin, who was a lawyer, was quick to carry out some fancy footwork that had John owning the flat, and Esther now had very little to her name. Even the roof over her head now depended on John to allow her and Daniel to stay, in addition to the bills that she had to pay.

Then one day, to her great surprise, Esther had a visit from her mother and Abena. They told her that John would be coming back to her for a trial period of two months.

It was the final humiliation.

Esther had lost her dignity, almost lost her faith and now she was being treated like some sort of criminal. Her heart was heavy and she felt the black cloud of depression deepen, but she agreed. Esther knew that her relationship with her mother depended on it. If she had refused she had no doubt that Ruth would have disowned her.

John moved back in swiftly. To Esther, it was torture, both mentally and physically, as she was sleeping in the rocking chair next to Daniel in his cot. She could not work out why John had agreed to the reconciliation since he clearly had no interest in trying to work things out. Instead, he insulted her and put her down every day, pushing her and banging up against her, anything that he could do to undermine her and make her feel worthless.

He brought friends around to make fun of her and despite the pastor visiting to speak to him no less than five times, John continued his cruelty towards her. Finally, one evening he said to her,

"Esther, I have been thinking about you while I was out," he shook his head, a mock look of regret on his face.

"I just do not know what I ever saw in you. Look at you, you're skinny, ugly, just revolting. Oh, and I've got news for you too, I don't love you, in fact I don't think I ever did!" He laughed a cruel laugh. "I'm off, and I won't be back. No one could expect me to live with such an ugly miserable bitch as you. They'll understand, in fact they all feel sorry for me." And with another cruel laugh he was gone.

Esther picked up her phone with tears streaming down her face, her hands trembling. She would send a message to Levi, ask him to take care of Daniel. She would wait around the corner to make sure that he came to get him and then she would go. It would soon be all over. She would soon be free of her torturous life.

Chapter Fourteen
Through the valley of death

Esther waited around the corner. She had Daniel's baby alarm with her, it was in range and she could hear her child sighing contentedly in his sleep. It seemed a very long time before she saw the familiar figure of Levi, his slight limp identifying him, walking out of the darkness, the key to her apartment block in his hand. As he passed under the light at the front of the building she could see that his face was etched with worry.

She tried to close her mind to the repercussions of what she planned to do. As the door closed behind Levi, she put the baby alarm in the lobby of the flats and went to her car. She had parked it away from the building so that it could not be seen from the flat. It had started to rain softly now and the shimmer on the windscreen made Esther think that the sky was crying with her. As always, even at night, the streets of London were busy and Esther inched along them. She had left her phone and everything she owned at home in her handbag. She did not want anyone to be able to contact her.

She slammed the brakes on just in time to avoid hitting the car in front that had stopped suddenly. She had to concentrate, but it was hard. In her mind voices and memories clamoured;

"Come on Esther, you can do it! Come to daddy!" Her infant self was smiling, arms outstretched as she took her first steps.

"Esther, your father has left, it's going to be just you and me and baby Levi from now on." Esther remembered the crippling grief she had felt, the emptiness that there had always been in her life where her father should have been.

"Well done Esther, you are top of the class – again!" Certificates from the many academic achievements through her life floated like confetti around in her mind.

"Hello Esther, my name is Lizzie!" Esther saw Lizzie's warm smile and thought she could not have had a better friend.

"Thank you Esther, you have made my time in the hospice a gentle and hopeful time," Esther cried harder as she thought

about the patients she had sat with and nursed in the hospice. She wished the memories would stop but they continued.

Now in her mind she could see herself sitting with Adam on the bench in front of the hospital, eating her lunch. She saw the little girl she had nursed in the hospital, and the many, many more patients that she had known during her nursing career.

Now as she drove, the scene in her mind changed and she saw herself in the desert Kingdom of Saudi Arabia and in the terrible conditions of the prison. She saw Malaya and then Huda and the people she had known there. She saw Hesham's kind face and even the terrible sight of Adam coming out of Lizzie's bedroom.

"Hi, I'm John," Esther's heart ached as she remembered the kind smile and the handsome face of the man who would, in the end, drive her to desperate action.

Esther saw the day in the park in Cornwall when John had proposed, the swirling autumn leaves always reminded her of that happy time.

Esther saw her son now, as a newborn infant, his first smile and then her brother's accident that had ended his career.

"Stupid cow!"
"Pathetic failure!"
"Miserable bitch!"
"Esther! I'm you mother and I'm telling you, you're wrong!"

The insults thrown at her by her husband and his family and even her own mother now rang in her ears as though they were in the car with her. Esther pulled over to the side of the road, clapping her hands over her ears to try and block out the sound of their harsh and cruel insults. She banged her head on the steering wheel and wailed.

Even God seemed to have deserted her. Her prayers had gone unanswered and he had done nothing to stop her husband and his family from driving her to this desperate, dark and lonely place. A passage she had learned from the bible came into her mind. The words of Jesus, suffering on the cross:

My God, my God, why hast thou forsaken me? Why art thou so far from helping me, and from the words of my roaring? O my God, I cry in the daytime, but you don't hear me; and in the night, and am not silent. But you are holy, O thou that inhabits the praises of Israel. Our fathers trusted in you: they trusted, and you delivered them. They cried unto you, and were delivered: they trusted in you, and were not confounded. But I am a worm, and no man; a reproach of men, and despised of the people.

All they that see me laugh me to scorn: they shoot out the lip, they shake the head, saying, He trusted on the Lord that he would deliver him: let him deliver him, seeing he delighted in him. But you took me out of the womb: you made me hope when I was upon my mother's breasts. I was cast upon thee from the womb: thou art my God from my mother's belly. Be not far from me; for trouble is near; for there is none to help. Many bulls have compassed me: strong bulls of Bashan have beset me round. They gaped upon me with their mouths, as a ravenous and roaring lion.

Esther had never felt more alone. She knew that what she was planning to do would condemn her to burn in hell, but her life was intolerable and she could stand it no more. Even her son, her precious Daniel was not enough to stop her. The thought of her child brought fresh tears. Suddenly there was a knock on the window. It was a police officer, his coat collar turned up against the rain.

"Are you alright miss?" He asked, "Have you broken down?"

"No, no I haven't." Esther sobbed.

"Well you are on double yellows and causing quite a tail back. Are you sure you're alright, where are you heading?"

"Um, The Tower Hotel," Esther said, then, "I'm fine, I just had some bad news, I'm sorry officer, I'll go."

"Well, if you're sure that you are ok?" The officer looked doubtful.

"Really, I'm fine," Esther forced a smile and wiped her eyes.

She was close now, the huge structure of Tower Bridge, lit up in the dark, came into view. Esther turned her car into the car park of the Tower Hotel and parked it.

***

Ruth was waiting anxiously for Levi when he returned with baby Daniel and a bag that Esther had packed for him. "What's going on Levi?" She asked, taking the child from him. Daniel was already asleep and he did not wake as Ruth put him down gently in the cot that he slept in when he was at his granny's house.

Levi shrugged. His face was a picture of concern; he had a very bad feeling that he was trying his best to ignore.

"There was nothing to see at the flat, except..."

"Except what?" Ruth said.

"Well her handbag was still there. I looked around outside and the car had gone but it looks like Esther didn't take anything else with her, wherever she has gone."

Ruth clasped her hands to her heart. A feeling of dread crept up, fanning out all over her body from her toes. Her daughter had been very unhappy, she knew that, and she knew that as her mother she had been less than sympathetic to her. She could not even allow the thought into her mind that Esther might be planning to..."

"Call the police Levi." Ruth said, through a mouth dry with fear.

"What?" Levi looked at his mother in alarm.

"CALL THE POLICE, NOW!" She shouted.

The police response was swift and an officer was soon at the house taking what details Ruth and Levi could give them. They seemed to think, like Ruth and Levi that Esther was planning to end her life.

"We'll put out an immediate alert to our officers to look out for the car and for your daughter and I'll stay here with you in case she should call." The woman police officer smiled kindly at them.

***

Esther walked slowly towards the bridge. It was busy, streams of traffic crossed both ways and a soft rain continued to fall. As she walked over the bridge, Esther looked down at the swirling blackness of the water below. Underneath that water was oblivion. It would be the end to her pain and suffering and the chance to sleep, forever.

Esther waited as a group of tourists passed her, talking in a language that she did not recognise. Their faces were lit up with the excitement of seeing this iconic landmark and the Tower of London illuminated in the night, ahead. How long had it been since Esther had felt the wonder and happiness that she saw on their faces? She could not remember.

Once they had passed, Esther quickly clambered up onto the broad railing of the bridge and sat for a moment, her legs dangling over the edge above the water, as she got her balance. Below her, the dark depths were beckoning. She knew that she had to be quick. Someone would see her and try to stop her if she waited. But Esther wanted to make one last prayer. She felt as far from God as she had ever felt, she felt abandoned and unloved, but she wanted to pray.

O my crucified Jesus, mercifully accept the prayer that I now make to thee for help in the moment of my death, when at its approach all my senses shall fail me. When my weary and downcast eyes can no longer look up to you, be mindful of the loving gaze which now I turn on you, and have mercy on me. When my parched lips can no longer kiss your most sacred wounds, remember then those kisses which now I imprint on you and have mercy on me.

When my cold hands can no longer embrace the cross, do not forget the affection with which I embrace it now, and have mercy on me. And when my swollen and lifeless tongue can no longer speak, remember that I called upon you now. Jesus to thee do I commend my soul. Amen

Esther was not sure that her payer would be answered or even heard. How far she had fallen from that bright girl of faith she had been. That seemed a lifetime ago. Suddenly through the drizzle she saw a gaggle of workers making their way home across the bridge, umbrellas raised. She swung her legs around and dropped down onto the bridge, just as they got to her. But their umbrellas were tilted towards Esther and they did not see her.

***

In his patrol car, a young officer heard the report giving the details of the car and young woman who was thought to be trying to harm herself, and swore to himself, under his breath. Immediately, he knew that the woman was the young motorist he had spoken to earlier, parked on double yellow lines and crying. When he had seen her, she was heading towards Tower Bridge, could she be planning to jump? He took off, sirens blaring towards the bridge. He just hoped that he would not be too late.

***

At home, Ruth was shivering uncontrollably. Levi was trying to comfort her but he was also deadly afraid that they might never see Esther again. How could he not have realised that she was so unhappy, so desperate that she would consider the ultimate sin, suicide?

"Shall I call John?" He asked tentatively.

Ruth spun round to face him. The scales were falling from her eyes and she realised now, that everything Esther had said about John was true. How could she have doubted her? She was Esther's mother!

"Yes, call him, he should know what he has done." She said, a cold edge to her voice.

Levi was confused but he made the call anyway, putting his phone to speakerphone.

John answered on the third ring.

"Hi, Levi my man! Whassup?" He said.

"It's Esther," Levi said fighting back tears. "She's gone."

"Gone? What d'you mean gone?"

"We think she's going to, to..." Levi stumbled over the words.

"Going to what? Where's Daniel?" John's voice was serious now.

"Daniel's here with us. We think that Esther might be going to kill herself," Levi said in a strangled tone.

"Oh come on, Levi, its not like you to be dramatic, you must be wrong, you must be." Levi told John what had happened in the last hour, including the fact that the police were looking for Esther.

John gave a low whistle. "So the old Bill are taking it seriously?"

"Yes they are." Levi said giving a half smile of apology to the police officer for the nickname John had used. "Maybe you should go out as well and look for her?"

"I wouldn't know where to look." John said, his tone almost casual. I'll come round to you and pick up Daniel."

Ruth grabbed Levi's arm almost making him drop the phone. She was shaking her head violently, mouthing 'no no NO!'

Now Levi was really confused. He made a gesture that said 'what can I do about it? I can't stop him.' and said into the phone.

"OK, John."

***

On the bridge Esther was ready. She had prayed for a sign and none had come. Clearly God had deserted her, had nothing further for her, and did not care if she left this earth. She began to stand up on the railing of the bridge. It was slick from the rain. She had taken her shoes and socks off and she was on bare feet. She could feel the rain falling on them and the vision of Jesus washing his disciples feet came to her mind.

Approaching Tower Bridge, the young police officer killed his siren and lights and drove slowly towards the woman he could see in the gloom, standing, swaying on the railing of the bridge. He drove as close as he could without alerting her to his presence and holding his breath, he opened the patrol car door and got out. The young woman was staring down into the water and was obviously about to jump. She did not see him approaching her.

***

John arrived at Ruth's house in ten minutes. The police officer there told him that they thought that his wife had been spotted and that they had an officer on scene.

"Did she say why?" John asked.

Ruth thought that was a strange thing for him to ask. What did it matter why? What mattered was that someone brought Esther back to them, safe. Ruth had a feeling of the deepest sadness, not just for her daughter's current danger but also for the fact that she had not been there when she needed her.

"Why are you asking that John?" She challenged her son in law. "Maybe its because *you* might be a big part of the reason she is so unhappy?"

"Ruth! You're upset so I will pretend you didn't say that." There was a hard edge to John's voice and Levi looked at this mother and John in confusion.

What was going on?

"OK, everyone, let just calm down," the policewoman stepped in now. "This is a stressful time for all of you and it's easy to get overwrought. Why don't you put the kettle on Ruth?"

Ruth went to the kitchen where she leaned on the work surface, her head in her hands, "Oh Esther, please darling, come back to us," she wept.

***

On the bridge Esther was ready. She was afraid but the thought that soon her pain would end was so enticing. She closed her eyes and bent her legs, letting go of the pillar beside her. For a moment she was airborne and weightless.

Suddenly she felt a hand around her ankle and Esther crashed painfully back into the outside of the railing.

"I've got you, don't struggle! Hold on, I'll pull you back over."

Esther stared down into the blackness below her and did as she was told. She felt a hand around her other leg and then the one voice was joined by others as she was pulled back over the railings and onto the bridge.

As soon as she was on her feet again she could see faces full of concern around her and a young policeman hurrying from his patrol car with a blanket that he threw around her. She recognised him immediately. Suddenly her heart was full of gratitude to him. God *had* sent her a sign, He had sent this unlikely angel to save her and she knew that she did not want to die anymore. She wanted to see Daniel, her mother, her brother, her friends, she wanted her life and she was going to fight for what she wanted. She was not going to let John or anyone else deter her from that.

"I think you've got a split lip and a bruise on your head from where you swung back into the bridge. I've called an ambulance." The young officer said. "We have an officer at your mother's house and she will tell your family which hospital you are going to.

Esther wanted to protest and say that she did not need to go to hospital but she kept her mouth shut. She would let this officer and the other people who wanted to help look after her. Esther was just glad to be alive.

Chapter Fifteen

The road from despair

Esther found herself on the way to hospital, despite her protests. As the ambulance doors closed, the last face she saw was the face of the young policeman. He smiled at her, giving her the thumbs up in encouragement, and Esther smiled back. She was glad he had saved her. She was.

She was seen in St Thomas's and then transferred to a psychiatric facility for evaluation. She found it healing to pour out all her troubles to a person who had no stake in what she said or felt, someone who would listen to her without judging. She was already regretting the trouble she had caused and could not wait to see Daniel and her mother.

She reflected that if any good had come from that terrible night, it was that she and her mother were now closer than ever. Her mother had visited with Daniel and Esther had held him to her, smelling his baby hair and crying tears of joy holding her mothers hand. Ruth wept her own tears for her daughter and the pain she had gone through, alone.

"Oh Esther, I am so sorry, I should have believed you, that man and his family are just beyond evil."

"Why do you say that? Has something happened?" Esther said.

"I am not sure I should tell you," Ruth waved her arm to encompass the room, "While you are in here, but I am so furious with John and his family. He is trying to excuse his despicable behaviour by saying…." Ruth's voice faltered.

"By saying what?" Esther demanded.

Ruth took a deep breath.

"By saying that you were cheating on him. He has even hinted that the reason you tried to commit…" Ruth could not say the word 'suicide' "…the reason you were so upset was because you had been found out, and that Daniel might not be his child."

Esther closed her eyes and shook her head. She would put nothing past John and she was not surprised that he had tried to take the attention back onto himself by playing the wronged husband.

"You know that it's all lies, right?"

"Of course I do my darling," Ruth squeezed her hand. "Oh, look at your poor face, you are black and blue and your lip looks painful."

Esther touched her lip. Her cuts and bruises would heal but she was not so sure about her heart.

Levi came to visit her the next day, full of fury at their mother for not believing Esther when she told her what John was doing to her.

"How can a mother take her son in laws side over her daughter?" He raged.

From idolising John, Levi now hated him with a passion that frightened Esther. She knew that there was going to have to be a lot of bridge building for them all. She trusted that they would pull through it.

A saying she knew came to her mind. It was very true and something that she had learned in therapy.

Many people love the idea of you but lack the maturity to handle the reality of you.

Satisfied that she was much improved, Esther was discharged and went back to the flat. Everything was as she had left it that night and for a moment the ghost of the despair she had felt swept through her. Daniel seemed delighted to be back and Esther busied herself dusting and cleaning and changing the beds. Things were going to be very different now.

A meeting was arranged between the two families two weeks after Esther was discharged. Ruth did not want Esther to go but Esther insisted. She wanted to show John that she was strong and not afraid of him, although that was not really how she felt.

The meeting was held in a terrible atmosphere. Levi was still barely speaking to his mother and John could not look any of them in the eye. As usual, Abena took the floor. To anyone listening it would seem that John was the injured party. Esther kept her temper under control as she listened to the list of grievances that had been made up by John's family.

Abena cried crocodile tears and hinted that Esther might have some mental condition that had made it impossible for her to be a good wife. John, when questioned by a furious Levi, stood by his story that he thought that Esther had been unfaithful to him. He cited her work colleague Chris Walker, although he added that he was sure there had been others before him.

Esther listened, her face impassive. She would not give John or his family the satisfaction of seeing how horrified and hurt she was by their ridiculous suggestions.

Ruth, who was well respected at church, had a lot of support from the elders of the church and all of them were appalled at how John's family was behaving. Esther took great comfort from that.

After the meeting, it was agreed that Esther and John should divorce. Esther was proud of her family for the way that they had maintained their dignity during the horrible meeting with John's family. Esther felt a satisfaction that the rest of the community seemed to have realised what the truth of the matter was and a bit of what she had to put up with all the time she had been with John.

Ruth had decided that they should go back home to Ghana for a visit and Esther was relieved to be getting out of London. That her mother and Levi were going with her seemed like a great way to mend the rift that had been between her and her mother and between Levi and Ruth.

Esther had spent a long time with the pastor talking over what had happened and he had gently led her back to the home that she had treasured for so long - her faith. As she considered her future as a divorced woman, Esther felt a mixture of relief and failure. Her heart was still very badly bruised by the traumatic time that she had gone through. She read something that sustained her in the darkest hours, during the times that she felt that no one would ever love her again, that she was unattractive and useless.

My next relationship will be my last, so I'm not worried and I'm not rushing. I want this love to find me, learn me, want me, need me and love me in slow motion. We have forever to go!

It was true that the next love she fell for would have to be chosen with care. She had Daniel to think about now. Any man in her life would be in his life too and that was a big space to fill.

The holiday in Ghana was just what everyone needed. On the flight over, the three adults were quiet, only Daniel giggled with excitement and made himself a favourite with the cabin crew with his smiles and gurgles. As Esther held him to the window, he clapped his hands and said "oooh" over and over again, his eyes wide with delight, as he looked out at the fluffy clouds.

The warm welcome that awaited them from the minute they stepped off the plane was almost overwhelming. Daniel was pounced on as though he was a tasty morsel for a starving pride of lions and was kissed and hugged and admired wherever they went. Esther got used to him being taken from her and soon learned to relax amongst people who were so open-hearted and clearly delighted to welcome them home. The family was determined that as well as pampering their guests and arranging trips to the beach, Levi and Esther should learn something about the culture that they had never experienced as children.

As she had lived all her life in the UK, Esther had not really thought much about her African heritage. Esther and Levi learned about Dr. Kwame Nkrumah who bravely and successfully fought for Ghana's independence, and was the first African leader to do that. They also learned that many of the slave castles built had been erected in Ghana. With Ruth and other members of what was a huge family, they visited the Kwame Nkrumah mausoleum, W.E.B. Dubois Centre, the Cape Coast Castle, Elmina Castle and Assin Manso, an important place that had been the last bathing site.

Esther had always seen herself as a Black British citizen and very far removed from Africa in every respect – geographically, culturally and spiritually. But now, she began to see herself as an African British citizen, and she saw the value of being African. She discovered that her history did not begin with the scourge and abomination of slavery but with ancestors who built incredible monuments, who ruled for thousands of years and whose influence has enriched many modern-day religions.

One night under a star-strewn sky, Levi Ruth and Esther sat on the veranda of the family beach house. Recognising that they needed some time to themselves, their hosts had left them there for the weekend. As Esther swung on a porch swing, she could hear the waves crashing on the shore and after a day spent playing in the shallows, Daniel was fast asleep.

"This is heaven." Ruth said. "The three people I love most in the world with me in such a lovely place."

Levi had been very quiet around his mother since Esther's suicide attempt but now he opened up and said,

"Pity you never really told us much about our history." His tone was accusatory and Esther sighed. She had forgiven her mother, why couldn't Levi?

"I'm sorry son, I didn't know that you were interested."

"Like you didn't know that your precious son in law was a liar and a bastard?" He spat.

"Levi, I'm so sorry and I will never forgive myself for being taken in by John and his family, but if your sister can find peace with me why cant you?"

"I think I know why." Esther went to sit by her brother and put her arm around him.

"You are so disappointed that John fooled you too." Levi opened his mouth to speak and Esther put her hand up to silence him.

"I know that you did not know what was going on in the same way that mum did but I also know how manipulative John can be. But you have to believe me, Levi, when it comes to you; I know that he really loved you. He was so devastated when you broke your leg. His feelings for you were genuine, and it was because of that I didn't say anything to you. Look at it from mum's point of view. John was really good to you, because he genuinely loved you like a brother and she did not want to think that my marriage would go the same way as hers did. Can't you understand that?"

Levi shrugged.

"But how can a mother take the side of *anyone* over their own child?" He said angrily.

Ruth was crying softly now and Esther took both of her brother's hands in hers.

"Please Levi, let it go, we need to get past this now because I am quite sure that John and his family have not finished with us yet. They have been shown up for what they are as a family and now John is like a cornered rat, he will lash out for sure. We still have to get the divorce over with and we need to stick together for that. Please Levi?"

For a moment, Levi was quiet and all they could hear were the waves and the lanterns on the veranda rattling as they swayed in the sea breeze, the candles in them sputtering.

Finally, with tears rolling down his cheeks he nodded. Esther hugged him to her. She knew that he had suffered bitter disappointment when his career as a footballer ended before it even began and that the loss of John and the realisation of what a monster he really was had hit him hard. Ruth got up from her seat and came over to them. Standing in front of her son, she tentatively held her arms out to him. For a moment he hesitated and then stood up and hugged his mother and sister with all his strength. Their tears mingled.

At last the wounds could begin to heal.

Esther's prediction that John would try to get revenge on her proved horribly accurate. She arrived back at the flat to find the locks changed. Standing outside with Daniel in her arms she knocked on the door. John answered it; she could smell the alcohol on his breath. She felt a deep disgust for him overwhelm her.

"Hey, Daniel, daddy's boy!" He slurred trying to take Daniel from Esther. Esther held on to the child who was reaching out, excited to see his father.

"Bitch!" He hissed at Esther.

"Well, see how you like this you cow. You're out of here, I've changed the locks and dumped your stuff in your mother's back garden!" He slammed the door and from inside Esther could hear women laughing and loud music.

At their home, Ruth and Levi had discovered the soggy pile of Esther and Daniel's belongings that John had dumped in the back garden. Anything worth money had been taken and the rest of their belongings kicked around in the mud as opportunists had looked for anything worth taking.

Ruth dissolved into tears and Levi comforted her, fighting back his own tears.

"That bastard, I'll kill him!" He said picking up one of Daniels' favourite teddies, now limp and filthy with mud.

Levi tried to gather up what he could. He knew that Esther would be there soon; she and Daniel had obviously been thrown out of their home. Levi knew that his sister and John were buying the flat and he was afraid now that his sister might be swindled out of the home that Esther's money had paid for. He knew that one of John's cousins was a hotshot lawyer. He felt a feeling of dread creep over him.

By the time that Esther got to them, Ruth had put as much as she could in the washing machine. Esther wept as she realised that all her jewellery had gone, the jewellery box emptied and ground into the mud. Many precious things of hers and Daniels had been lost, forever.

Esther and Daniel were right that John would turn the divorce into an ugly battle. He did everything he could to get the house but showed no interest at all in offering any child support for his son. Esther was to find that any kind of process of that type was long-winded. In the meantime, she worked and she prayed and met a young preacher who had come to their church as a guest pastor.

The connection between Isaac and Esther was almost instant although there was no element of physical attraction to it. With patience, and infinite kindness, he coaxed Esther's deepest fears and pain out of her, he soothed her anger at her husband, telling her that she needed to leave all of that behind her. He prayed with her.

Dear Lord

Thank you for your gift of forgiveness. Your only Son loved me enough to come to earth and experience the worst pain imaginable so I could be forgiven. Your mercy flows to me in spite of my faults and failures. Your Word says to "clothe yourselves with love, which binds us all together in perfect harmony." Help me demonstrate unconditional love today, even to those who hurt me.

I understand that even though I feel scared, my emotions don't have to control my actions. Father, may Your sweet words saturate my mind and direct my thoughts. Help me release the hurt and begin to love as Jesus loves. I want to see my offender through my Saviour's eyes. If I can be forgiven, so can he. I understand there are no levels to your love. We are all your children, and your desire is that none of us should perish.

You teach us to "let the peace that comes from Christ rule in our hearts." When I forgive in words, allow your Holy Spirit to fill my heart with peace. I pray this peace that only comes from Jesus will rule in my heart, keeping out doubt and questions. And above all, I am thankful. Not just today, not just this week, but always. Thank you for the reminder, "Always be thankful." With gratitude I can draw closer to you and let go of unforgiveness. With gratitude I can see the person who caused my pain as a child of the Most High God. Loved and accepted. Help me find the compassion that comes with true forgiveness.

And when I see the person who hurt me, bring this prayer back to my remembrance, so I can take any ungodly thoughts captive and make them obedient to Christ. And may the confidence of Christ in my heart guide me into the freedom of forgiveness. I praise you for the work you are doing in my life, teaching and perfecting my faith. Amen

It was hard for Esther to open her heart and to pray for a man who had done so much to hurt her. Isaac prayed with her over and over again and slowly but surely she began to heal. As Esther told him about her life, he suggested that maybe she could think about writing a book to help get everything down on paper and release it from her heart.

Esther considered it. This could be the start of a new chapter for her. She decided that she would use her story to inspire others.

A new journey was about to begin.

Chapter Sixteen

Delivering the Dream

Despite the fact that her marriage had collapsed and John had taken all her money, Esther was more content than she had been in a long time. Back with her mother and Levi, she and Daniel enjoyed the love of family and Esther was free to come and go to her work while Ruth was delighted to play the doting grandmother. Esther enjoyed her regular meetings with pastor Isaac and drew great strength from him.

At work, Chris continued to support her and to help her explore the arena she felt so passionately about. Esther could tell that her mother was having a very hard time coming to terms with what had happened and she tried to be as gentle as she could with her. Pastor Isaac saw them both together as well as seeing Esther on her own and his kindness and spiritual goodness helped the whole family, even Levi who, although he pretended not to want to be part of their spiritual coaching, always seemed to be somewhere nearby when the pastor called.

Lizzie came back to the UK and was utterly appalled at what had happened to her friend. Hugging Esther so close that Esther could hardly breathe, Lizzie wept with her. When Esther told her that all the savings she had accumulated in Saudi Arabia and even the flat she had been buying with John had gone, leaving her with nothing, Esther thought that her friend would explode. It was all she could do to stop Lizzie from going around to confront John.

The friends sat together in Esther's room and for a while it felt like it had been when they were student nurses together. They cried, then laughed, and they hugged and remembered old times. The day they had met, their times nursing together in Saudi Arabia. Their children loved each other, Tessa bossed little Daniel around and he doted on her, seeing her as an older sister.

Esther had not seen Adam for years. His parents had moved to Australia and he spent his holidays there, with them. Now Lizzie told Esther that he would be coming to the UK for a conference in a month and he hoped that she would agree to meet him.

"Of course!" Esther said, "Silly man, all that is ancient history now!"

Esther was a lot happier now at work, she felt able to really devote herself to the important work that was being done and Chris was a constant friend and help to her, bringing her up to speed with the projects the agency was working on at any time. She had dropped out of her studies during all of her trials but now she had applied to the university and been accepted to further her studies. She would finally get the qualifications that she wanted. Her life was getting back on track. It was a slow process, but Esther could see the light at the end of the tunnel.

And another miracle had occurred. Esther had met someone else. She had kept him at arms length initially, terrified of making another mistake. From time to time she would see John out and about with his new fiancé who had been chosen for him by his parents, or so Esther thought. They would have no one to blame when it all went wrong.

And it would, Esther was sure of that. Her sessions with pastor Isaac had taught her to hope for the best for her enemies and she did for John and especially the woman she was now engaged to, but it was difficult sometimes. If they did meet he would blank her and make a great show of being overly demonstrative to his fiancé.

To Esther she looked like a quiet woman, a woman easily pushed around by John and his family. As her strength and her energy returned, Esther lived by the sayings;

I can and I will – watch me!
I wake up with determination and go to bed with satisfaction

The wounds were healing and Esther was taking care of her physical health as well. She went to the gym and ate well and for the first time in a long time, she felt her spirit rise. She learned to enjoy the little things in life and to take pleasure from simple enjoyments like walking in the park with Daniel and decorating the Christmas tree as a family. John was continuing his accusations that Daniel was not his son and Esther tried not to let anger towards him overwhelm her. He demanded a paternity test and then failed to turn up for testing.

The new man in Esther's life, Mark, was kind and considerate and most importantly patient. Mark himself had been through a similar painful divorce and had come out the other side, obviously scathed but willing to start anew. Now he gave all his support to Esther, propping her up when she felt weak and making sure that when she was down he lifted her with a little surprise or even just a smile. Esther felt herself falling for this strong and kind man, who was in all aspects the opposite of John.

At times she still felt that all Ghanaians were against her. She would hear them whispering about her in the street when she met members of Johns' family and friends. Mark was there when she faltered, and Isaac made sure that she was fed spiritually.

Money was a big worry for Esther. Since John had taken everything she had and everything she had worked so hard for, she had no idea how she was going to fund her study. The job she had, while it was fulfilling, saw her working part-time and in an intern position. It was not enough to pay her tuition fees and set up a home for her and Daniel.

It worried her a lot and it occupied her mind and kept her from having peaceful sleep. She knew that her mother loved having her and Daniel at home with her but now that she felt stronger she needed to be independent. She was a mother and she needed to set up a home with her son.

On a cold afternoon, she and Daniel went to the park with Levi. She had been hoping it would snow so that Daniel could experience the magic of snowfall for the first time in his life. The skies were leaden but no snow fell as they played on the swings and then holding his nephew's hands and with his little feet resting on his own, Levi shuffled around kicking a football, as Daniel squealed with pleasure. Esther felt love for her son and her brother overwhelm her. Peace was returning to her soul.

The next time that she saw pastor Isaac she confided in him about the worries she had about money. He smiled at her in the way that always soothed her.

"Esther, you need to pray and to turn your worries over to the Lord. He has his plan for you and he will make sure that you have all you need to fulfill your destiny in life." Esther smiled back at him. She knew that she had to be patient and believe that God would provide.

A month after Lizzie had gone back to Saudi, Adam arrived. Esther felt nervous to see him after all this time. The last time she had seen him – well, that was best forgotten! They met at the hospital. The course was being held there and they arranged to meet on the bench that they had sat on together, all those years ago.

Esther got there first and sat down. It was a far cry from the summer day when they had talked while she ate her lunch and that seemed like a lifetime ago now. As Adam approached, she recognised him instantly. He had a bit more grey hair and was wrapped up against the cold of the December day but he was still the man she remembered who used to give her butterflies in her tummy. She got up and they hugged. Adam held her at arm's length and looked at her.

"Well for someone who has been through the mill you are looking pretty damn good!" He said.

"Thanks Adam!" Esther laughed.

Instantly any awkwardness was gone and they started to chat. On his phone, Adam showed her the latest pictures from Saudi of Tessa playing in the pool and Esther showed him the pictures of Daniel playing football in the park, with a lot of assistance from Levi.

"Esther, there is something I need to tell you. I want you to hear me out and not interrupt. Most of all I want you to be gracious."

Esther looked at him, puzzlement on her face.

"I don't understand, gracious, what do you mean by that?"

"You'll see." He said. "So are we in agreement, no interruptions?"

"OK, I guess so!" Esther laughed.

"Right. The fact is that there are people in Saudi Arabia who remember you and your kindness to them. They remember the way you helped them and the way you helped others. They ask Lizzie and me about you all the time and we have told them what has happened to you."

Esther looked dismayed, but Adam held his hand up.

"Esther you mustn't mind, these are people who love you, who would never judge you and who want the best for you. Just like you didn't judge them and opened your heart to them when the situation was reversed." John raised his eyebrows in inquiry and Esther hesitated and then nodded, almost imperceptibly.

"Anyway, they wanted you to know that they are thinking about you and they sent you this." From his inside pocket Adam took out an envelope and held it out to Esther. As he did, snow started to fall softly around them.

For a moment Esther kept her hands in her lap. Hesitantly, she raised her hand and took the envelope. She put her hand back in her lap, still holding the envelope.

"Open it," John said gently.

With tears in her eyes, Esther opened the envelope. Inside was a cheque.

She looked up at Adam. Tears were streaming down her cheeks.

"I can't..." she started but Adam put his hand gently on her arm.

"You can and you will Esther."

Esther looked down at the cheque again. Even though her tears, she could see that the number there would be what she needed to set up her own place again. It would cover her university fees too. It was the best Christmas present that anyone could ever give her and her heart ached with gratitude.

Adam gently took her hands in his.

"You know that old saying, 'What goes around comes around?' Well, I think this is evidence of that, don't you?"

Esther smiled at him through her tears and as he hugged her she laid her head on his shoulder. After all the pain and all the hurt, the despair and the misery, God was showing her that there were people who loved her, who wanted her to succeed. A saying popped into her mind. It was something that she had read and hoped it was true. Now it seemed it was!

Don't chase love, money or success. Become the best version of yourself and those things will chase you.

Esther could barely find the words to express her gratitude. The snow fell harder and Adam hugged her goodbye. As he disappeared into its swirls, Esther walked away, her head held high, snowflakes glistening in her hair, like a thousand diamonds. God had shown her what her future should be and He was ready to go and fulfill His purpose for her.

This is it, she said to herself as she walked towards home. This is it. Then stretching out her arms to the sky and whirling round and round in the snow, Esther shouted out loud.

Thank you Lord, I am ready to live My Dream!

Chapter Seventeen

Dear reader

You might have guessed that the story you have just read is based a lot on facts. There is a fair amount of fiction in there as well but the real and important truth of what I hope you have enjoyed reading, is that you should never give up on your dream.

Faith played a strong part of what sustained Esther and that is something that is important to me too. But even without that, there must always be a vision that is unwavering and which is the thing that you see on the back of your eyelids, every time that you close your eyes.

You get what you focus on, so focus on what you want.

There can be times in everyone's life when things look hopeless and it seems that however hard you try, you are treading water. Those are the times when you need to hold the tightest to your vision even when the waves of indecision and doubt seem about to overwhelm you. Take time to think about what that vision is:

Decide what you want
Write it down
Make a plan
Work on it every day

It might seem difficult and there will be times that you lose sight of your dream or are tempted to dilute it, just to make it easier to achieve. Don't! Even if it takes longer, even if you need to change direction slightly, do not compromise on what you want for yourself. If you have taken the time to formulate your dream then it is definitely worth sacrificing for.

The distance between
Where you are and where
You want to be is not as
Far as you think

The way that you think is as important as having the right mental attitude towards what you are trying to achieve. Take time and be still to think about what it is you are aiming for. Do not compromise if you are certain. Just follow your heart and you will get there. Be sure though, not to over promise yourself and set goals that are clearly unattainable. Your mind is your greatest weapon in your journey towards your dream.

I changed my thinking
It changed my life

There will always be people who, like boulders rolling down a hill towards you, are not only determined to make you change your course or squash your dreams but also to ruin you completely. We all know the type. The smiling girlfriend who, when we are trying to lose weight, offers us a cream cake and tells us "just one won't hurt."

The problem is that one leads to two and before you know it you are off the rails and all your hard work is undone. The same goes for any other dreams that you have in life. It is important to have the right support network around you. People who will encourage you and recognise the effort you are making and will stand proudly beside you when you achieve your dream.

Spend time with people
Who are good for your mental health.

On your journey, there will be a lot of obstacles to confront and there will be a lot of times when you will doubt yourself and what you are trying to do for yourself. While you are on your journey, life will go on around you and your life will continue with all the boring and mundane things that you have to do every day. Events might overtake you and make you doubt, things might be thrown in your way that make you want to rethink, but stay strong and use whatever you need to keep you on track. Most importantly, remember the old adage K.I.S.S. – Keep it simple, stupid!

Overthinking is the art of creating
Problems that don't exist!

On the subject of keeping things simple, there is a danger in being too ambitious too early. Don't confront yourself with goals that you cannot hope to achieve. Start with realism and a plan. Aiming too high, too early will only derail your efforts and you may never get back on track again. Use every support and encouragement that comes your way and you will soon be flying!

Start where you are
Use what you have
Do what you can

While you are on your journey to reach your dream you can use other people to lean on, to offer you support and to cheer you on. Be open and share what you are trying to do. You will soon find out who your real friends are. People who love you will want you to succeed as much as you do. But even though you might have support ultimately, this is your dream and your journey and you have to keep these words in mind:

Only I can change my life
No one can do it for me

For Esther, shame about what was happening in her life was something that often held her back. It might be that you are coming from a similar place where you feel ashamed of the things that have happened in your life, whether or not they were your fault. You need to put these thoughts behind you.

Don't be ashamed of your story
It will inspire others

There will be times when you do not succeed, that you need to re-group and try again. It is very easy at those times to think that it is pointless trying to go on. When you come to those times, do not give up. Keep going and remember that:

*Failure does not mean the game is over
It means try again with experience.*

*You are fearfully and wonderfully made,
If you want a situation to change it will change, only if
you believe.*

'What is your dream?'

Decide what you want
Write it down
Make a plan
Work on it everyday

References:

1. Dr. Monroe motivational speeches on youtube.
2. The Bible (New King James Version)
3. Thinkgrowprosper (instagram page)
4. T.D. Jakes' motivational speeches on youtube.
5. Purpose driven Life (Rick Wallen)
6. The good quotes - motivational quotes
7. Simple Nourished living quotes - motivational quotes
8. Shinzoo - motivational quotes
9. Quatations and Quotes - motivational quotes
10. Redsnapper-lanta.com - motivational quotes
11. Good day quote - motivational quotes
12. The curate collaborative - motivational quotes
13. Ink toner store blog - motivational quotes
14. Allfourvegan - instagram

BV - #0065 - 080222 - C0 - 203/127/9 - PB - 9781912092536 - Matt Lamination